SHADOW OF THE STAR DRAGON

AN EARTH FORCE SKY PATROL FILE: SOLAR YEAR 2388

BLAZE WARD

Shadow of the Star Dragon
An Earth Force Sky Patrol File: Solar Year 2388
Blaze Ward
Copyright © 2019 Blaze Ward
All rights reserved
Published by Knotted Road Press
www.KnottedRoadPress.com

ISBN: 978-1-64470-056-3

Cover art:
ID 23003822 © diversepixel | DepositPhoto.com

Cover and interior design copyright © 2019 Knotted Road Press

Never miss a release!
If you'd like to be notified of new releases, sign up for my newsletter.

I will never spam you, or use your email for nefarious purposes. You can also unsubscribe at any time.

http://www.blazeward.com/newsletter/

The Jessica Keller Chronicles

Auberon

Queen of the Pirates

Last of the Immortals

Goddess of War

Flight of the Blackbird

The Red Admiral

St. Legier

Winterhome

CS-405

Queen Anne's Revenge

Packmule

Persephone

Additional Alexandria Station Stories

The Story Road

Siren

Two Bottles of Wine with a War God

The Science Officer Series

The Science Officer

The Mind Field

The Gilded Cage

The Pleasure Dome

The Doomsday Vault

The Last Flagship

The Hammerfield Gambit

The Hammerfield Payoff

Earth Force Sky Patrol

Birth of the Star Dragon

Flight of the Star Dragon

Call of the Star Dragon

Shadow of the Star Dragon

Trial of the Star Dragon

Other Science Fiction Stories

Myrmidons

Moonshot

Menelaus

Earthquake Gun

Moscow Gold

Fairchild

White Crane

***The Collective* Universe**

The Shipwrecked Mermaid

Imposters

IMPOSTER

OF ALL THE things Royston Loughty had steeled himself to believe about the young woman seated across from him, wearing an Earth Force Sky Patrol Women's Auxiliary uniform no less, that she was an alien police officer, something akin to an Earth Force Sky Patrol agent, like disappeared Gareth, simply was so far down the list of possibilities that he would have discounted it utterly.

And yet.

She called herself Fatima Darzi, after the woman she was impersonating, the niece of his dear, old friend, the physicist Farouz Darzi, killed eleven years ago in a speeder accident. Outwardly, she even looked human enough. At least, until Pippa had removed the supposedly-Persian woman's hijab to reveal…

Tentacles.

As though Medusa herself were come down to turn him to stone. Perhaps that would have been the better outcome, if the rest of what she spoke was the truth. That there were aliens out there, living in mortal fear of humans gaining access to any kind of stardrive that would let them escape the sub-light travel limitations of Einsteinian physics.

That Royston Loughty, PhD, WMU, FRS, CBE, CStJ might have sealed someone's irrevocable doom. That his arrogance had pushed the galaxy to the edge of perhaps *xenocide*. He should have been smarter than that. He was, after all, a Doctor of Physics and the principle stellar radiation expert in the entire Solar System. Warden of the Mathematical Union. Fellow of the Royal Society. Commander, British Empire. Commander, Order of St John.

And fool. There was always that, if what Fatima said was true.

Royston lowered the pistol he had been holding on the stranger and clicked the safety on, quickly placing it back into the top drawer of his desk. He nodded to Pippa's arched eyebrow and she returned to the seat she had had taken earlier, pausing only to politely hand Ms. Darzi the cloth of her now-removed hijab, a lovely peach silk.

"So we are to believe her then, father?" Pippa asked. She paused and turned back to the stranger. "By what name should we address you?"

"It would be for the very best if you continued to refer to me as Fatima Darzi," the woman, this Grace woman said rather politely, in that soft burr of a Persian accent she affected. "If news gets out beyond this room, the First Inspector and the *Accord* Commission may feel that they have no choice but to move to extraordinary judgments."

Royston was fascinated by her sensory tentacles, even as her words struck him to the quick. They looked like nothing so much as short, dusky snakes extruded from her scalp, with a ring of lighter-colored spots near the ends, that somehow reminded him of eyes, just back from a larger such *eye* at the tip.

Alien. Here, in his office aboard Earth Force's L2 base, **The Arsenal**. As far as he knew the most secure facility in the Solar System.

"What happens if your superiors do panic?" Royston forced himself to speak past the sudden lump that had taken up residence in his throat.

"There was talk of a bio-weapon capable of inflicting xenocide, but hopefully just limiting it to humanity, if I understand the human term correctly," the Grace woman replied. "We had no such word in our language as *xenocide*, so we have had to borrow yours. As we have with many such barbaric, linguistic aberrations."

"Aberrations?" Pippa inquired, sounding like a scholar who read Tacitus in the original Latin.

"War is unknown in the *Accord of Souls*, Ms. Loughty," Darzi turned her head that way. The tentacles appeared to be sniffing the air like a cat seeking treats. "Violence exists nowhere on a scale that humans everyday seem to take for granted."

"What is the *Accord of Souls*?" Pippa pressed.

Royston sat back and listened, trying to pass a camel through the eye of a needle in his mind to find a way out of this impasse.

"The collective of species that the Chaa uplifted, fifty thousand of your years ago, before they left to seek the Creator," Darzi explained in words that left Pippa apparently as breathless as Royston. "Seventeen species, psionically bound together into a greater whole, conducting art, commerce, and joy."

"Why did these gods, the Chaa you called them, skip humanity?" Royston asked, intently.

Fifty millennia was a great span, but modern humans had already emerged as an intelligent, tool-using, language-using species by then. Even distant, galactic gods should have noticed.

"You have touched on one of the great philosophical and ethical conundrums of the current age, Dr. Loughty." Darzi actually smiled at him. Even her tentacles seemed to convey amusement. "We cannot know without asking them, but they fixed the other many species into their current forms and departed, apparently to seek the *Face of God*."

Good. At least the aliens still had some solid religion to ground them. Royston had always feared that a true atheism, as had been attempted a few times in the early periods of the Industrial Age, would tear all societies apart eventually. If they had Gods, they still had the opportunity for wonder and doubt. As well as a dread of ultimate consequences behind their behavior.

"And the *Accord of Souls* fears humanity? Correct?" Royston pursued an earlier comment.

"Yours is considered the single most violent, most dangerous species in the galaxy, Dr. Loughty," her voice turned serious. "Escaping your home system puts every other species in the universe at risk."

He couldn't really argue with that logic. Even a casual study of human history would bear out what a barbaric species they really still were.

"And your mission was to penetrate Earth Force, and Sky Patrol, and do what, Ms. Darzi?" Royston brought things back to a head.

She was an admitted imposter. An infiltrator. He

had only her word for anything, and her supposed knowledge of things from Gareth Dankworth, hopefully. If there was a better man in the Solar System, Royston Loughty had yet to meet him.

"I am a scout, Dr. Loughty," she shrugged in a most human manner. "I was to find out what you had accomplished, and how it might be derailed before it grew out of control."

There. Those were apparently the table stakes they would have to play, but Royston had somehow known that as soon as this woman removed her hijab and revealed the stark, mind-shattering truth.

"Then you have already failed, Ms. Darzi," Royston concluded dispassionately. "The knowledge exists within certain circles, and can thus never be contained again. Humans are like that. Having proven that it was possible, it is only a matter of time before the next scholar figures out how it was done, and improves upon my work. Even if I were to inject my own failures into future experiments, it would only delay the inevitable. How do we convince your superiors not to destroy humanity?"

"Why should we?" Darzi challenged him.

It was a telling, near-mortal blow.

"Because of Gareth," Pippa spoke up firmly. "Because you know him, or at least know of him, so you know what kind of man he is."

"Indeed, Ms. Loughty, but there is also Maximus," Darzi replied. "The criminal who was once Marc Sarzynski."

Pippa gasped and her hands flew to her mouth. Royston felt his heart begin to pound hard enough that it might rattle its way out of his chest. He paused for a moment to find the words.

"I had a theory that someone in the *Accord* had opened a wormhole in space for the purpose of kidnapping Gareth Dankworth, the same as they had previously done to Marc," Royston fought to keep his tone on this side of fear and anger. "Is that the truth?"

"It is, Dr. Loughty, but not in ways you could imagine," she said.

Quickly, the alien woman related the whole story, or at least the bits she had been cleared to know by her superiors. Sarzynski being captured by a crime boss looking for an assassin, failing to understand he could not subsequently control a man like that. Royston was especially thrilled with the bit about the two, tiny lizardmen, *Yuudixtl*, who took it upon themselves to find the *Accord of Souls* a guardian angel in the form of Gareth.

And then she came to the next part, even more unbelievable than the rest.

"Could you repeat that, Ms. Darzi," Royston said. "He was transformed into a what?"

"They call it a Star Dragon, Dr. Loughty," she shrugged. "I have never seen it, but I have heard rumors and stories, that he could transform from his new, Vanir form apparently into a giant, fire-breathing, flying lizard form."

Pippa had fallen utterly silent. Royston turned to her just to make sure his daughter was still breathing. Her eyes were pools of dread midnight. Perhaps this Grace woman was a medusa, and had transformed his daughter to alabaster.

"And a Vanir?" Royston asked.

"Seven foot some tall and three hundred plus pounds, by human reckoning," Darzi continued.

"The face is more angular than humans, and the eyes larger. They have ears that come to pronounced points, perhaps twenty percent larger than yours. Sarzynski is functionally identical, from a physical standpoint, without the secondary transformation."

"He's no longer human?" Pippa managed to gasp in a whisper.

"He is not, Ms. Loughty," Darzi said. "I'm sorry. It is my understanding that he refers to you even now as his betrothed."

That brought a splash of color to his daughter's utterly pale cheeks. Only Royston knew that Gareth had been literally on his way to propose to Pippa on the night when he was taken by Morty and Xiomber, to use their names.

Could he call it their *Christian* names?

Apparently, even Yuudixtl career criminals could be rehabilitated.

That gave Royston a jolt so hard that both women turned to him with some alarm.

"Father?" Pippa asked weakly.

He smiled at her and then turned his terrible gaze on the imposter.

"We will use your cover story, Ms. Darzi," Royston announced forcefully. "At least as part of a larger cover-up that I will need to cause to come into being immediately."

"Dr. Loughty?" the imposter, the Grace woman, asked.

"I had been planning to take a short sabbatical, Ms. Darzi," Royston said. "To find a particular human group, musicians as you will, and see if they could help inspire me to even greater heights of scientific creativity than I had achieved thus far.

Pippa would have accompanied me, so you will be able to as well, with no scandal attached to either of our reputations."

Both women blushed at the same time and same rate. Apparently, it transcended species, so it was probably a factor of intelligence rather than biology.

"We will depart The Arsenal and return to the surface of the Earth, as I had intended," Royston continued. "In the course of actions, I will just drop off the face of the Earth, to use the colloquialism, while sending the occasional postcard to Alvin, that he does not grow concerned at my disappearance."

"I do not understand," Fatima Darzi's doppelgänger said plaintively.

"You will contact your superiors and endeavor to convince them to bring Pippa and I to wherever we may talk to Gareth and whoever else needs to be involved," Royston said with a firm smile.

"Father, that's insane," Pippa exclaimed.

"It is, indeed, daughter," he replied. "But if I am to be seeking the *Life Bohemian* to explore some new facet of my discovery, no other research will move forward, especially if I tell Alvin and Sir Westfield I originally miscalculated the risks of accidentally destroying the Earth with the wormhole generator I have built. That will buy us at least six months without question."

"And then what?" Darzi asked, leaning forward and eyes growing large.

"Then I have to figure out how to keep your superiors from destroying humanity, my dear."

AN ILL-MANNERED PATIENT

GARETH SIMPLY COULD NOT HELP himself this morning. He knew Talyarkinash meant well, but having to be fed by someone else, as if he was a helpless infant, had left Gareth grumpier than a wet hen. He waved the spoon away almost angrily.

The Nari woman leaned back and put down the bowl and spoon of stew she had been feeding him. Her whiskers twitched forward in alarm, as did her ears.

Gareth rested both of his cast-encrusted hands on the dining room table with probably more of a thump that was necessary.

"I'm sorry," Gareth managed to make his voice polite. "It's just too much this morning."

"Should I program the kitchen machine to deliver a liquid breakfast substitute with a straw?" she asked.

It helped that her voice contained no mockery. Gareth hated being helpless, even if modern, *Accord* medicine meant that his hands would be fully healed in days, rather than months. Both eyes this morning in the mirror had held only the faintest trace of raccoon patches, from the terrible bruising and cuts the fight with the killer androids had inflicted.

But his hands had simply been smashed too badly for mere splints. As it was, Talyarkinash had explained the month or more of physical therapy that would be necessary for him to play piano or guitar again.

"No," Gareth breathed in defeat. "I know I'm a bad patient. Being helpless to even feed myself was just too much this morning. And I realize that I should have been in bed for a fortnight after what happened, rather than two days. It's just…"

"You want to be out there with Baker and Grodray, chasing your old friend," she replied in a quiet, helpful tone.

"Stopping him from destroying the galaxy," Gareth sort of corrected her.

"I understand," Talyarkinash smiled up at him.

She was truly his closest friend in the entire galaxy these days. Nothing more than a friend, although he suspected she might have different desires deep down. He still held out hope that they could somehow reverse the entire process and turn him back into a human, that he could be sent home.

Pippa would wait for him. He knew that. Just as he would have waited for her. It would just take time.

A hatch opened and two new bodies tromped into the semi-private dining space where he and the Nari doctor were seated.

"Hey, kid," Morty exclaimed, carrying a booster block over to the chair next to him and climbing up to sit at the table. With the extra height, he was nearly on a level with Talyarkinash. "Doc Fitzroy said you were down."

Xiomber ended up on the other side. Both of the tiny Yuudixtl were drinking coffee this morning, although Morty had somehow managed to add nearly a dram of brandy to his from the smell.

Of course, Gareth didn't suppose anyone but him might smell it. Talyarkinash, perhaps, if she got close enough.

Gareth held out both hands, like boxing gloves in the rigid casts.

"Overly grumpy, yes," Talyarkinash informed the table with a smile. "Forcible inactivity apparently is contrary to his very nature."

"Yeah, not surprising," Xiomber chirped. "Kinda why we picked him the first place."

"So I have a theory, Gareth," Morty grinned. "Goes back to the weird shit we had to do to reprogram you in the first place. Talyarkinash probably knows most of it, but maybe not the weird bits."

"Weird bits, you scaly reprobate?" the Nari woman turned her stern look and chuckles on the other two scientists. "What have you done now?"

"*Reformed* reprobates, I'll have you know, madam," Xiomber interjected tartly. "We have been adjudicated guilty and are currently serving our debt to society, thank you very much."

"Yes," she retorted with a sarcastic grin. "You seem so humble and reformed."

"So I got to thinking last night, when Fitzroy told us how bad Gareth got hamburgered on his recent mission," Morty said. "Couple of days of healing would be a really good thing, just so the body got over the shock, but we might be able to radically reduce the rest of his down time."

"How?" Gareth's cry was almost savage. Both Yuudixtl leaned back a notch. "Sorry."

"So if you ate a whole bunch of protein this morning, we might be able to convince Fitzroy to remove the casts," Morty said. "Then you go into full Star Dragon mode. The transformation has reshaping built right into it, so it ought to fix your hands, for the most part. Again, there's gonna be a crapton of pain, like you broke them both again, and it won't fully heal them. Soft tissue will need another week to recover. You game?"

"What does Talyarkinash need to feed me?" Gareth asked so intently that the other three laughed. "I'll be the best little chick ever, waiting to be fed. Anything to get out of these casts."

"It'll hurt, Gareth," Xiomber reminded him. "Things out of alignment now get forced back into shape. That means tearing and breaking."

"And?" Gareth smiled brittlely at the man.

"Make sure they take him someplace up in the mountains," Morty suggested to Talyarkinash as she picked up the bowl and spoon again. "And stay away from avalanche zones."

Outside the base, most of this hemisphere of *Irron* was in the depths of winter. The mountains reminded Gareth of family vacations to Colorado when he was a kid, especially the snow.

But to have his own hands back???

"Sign me up," Gareth pronounced, letting the Nari woman stuff a spoonful of stew into his mouth happily.

"Gotcha, kid," Morty suddenly hopped back down onto the floor and grabbed his lift. "I'll tell Doc Fitzroy you're in."

Xiomber joined him and the two departed.

"Better?" Talyarkinash asked as she filled the spoon again.

"I make a lousy patient, Talyarkinash," Gareth said. "As you have seen. Every minute I'm here is another minute Sarzynski has to perfect whatever plans he has , whatever trouble is coming."

Nobody knew Marc Sarzynski better than Gareth. They had been best friends for almost a decade, going back to ground school together. Until Marc turned to darkness when Pippa chose Gareth instead.

Dr. Loughty had once predicted that worlds would fall in their ensuing feud. But even that worthy had no idea just how right he had been.

DESPERATE MEASURES

BECAUSE MARC SARZYNSKI worked hard at being ruthless, he had developed an instinct for when to cut and run. It had saved his ass more than once, when the Constables had gotten a solid-enough lead to come knocking. When a Heavy Team kicked in the door to Gonquah's estate, the Th'Tarni man had been arrested almost without incident, but Marc have moved his base of operations absolutely immediately.

Several people in his gang had expressed surprise, but Zorge had just nodded and gone along without question, packing what he could and burning the rest.

Two days later, another Heavy Team had shown up at the resort Marc had been renting in the off-season, but he was already gone by then, leaving only one supposedly-innocent watcher to identify everything. The rest of the gang had been extra quiet after that.

They didn't understand violence, but that was because they were of the *Accord of Souls*. Even most of his gang still had some level of empathy with their fellows, broken though it might be. Marc was human, in spite of his exterior shell as a Vanir. He could kill anybody and everybody that got in his way.

Marc finished reading the details from his watcher's report. Sloppy, on the part of the Constables, but they hadn't brought a Star Dragon with them. Gareth would have made different suggestions about the approach.

That man understood how to kick in a door shooting.

Maybe he had been as grievously injured as one of Marc's moles still hiding in the Constabulary had suggested, from medical reports the woman had seen.

A knock at the hatch brought Marc's eyes up.

"Enter," he called.

The team was currently *seeing the galaxy*, as the old saw went. They had rented a long-term transport pod in which to stay, as they rode in between worlds on a cargo vessel. Technically, Marc owned the entire vessel around them, through a series of corporate shells he had inherited when he took over the gang by killing Cinnra, back on *Zathus*.

For now, they could travel incognito, hidden among a thousand other such containers in the big ship's belly. It would also let them visit any planet along the itinerary, as long as they didn't stay more than a day or two during the loading and unloading process.

Zorge opened the hatch and stepped in, closing it

behind him. There were ten people with them right now, so the pod could be a little crowded, but nobody was complaining. Jail cells would be even smaller spaces to be confined in.

"We'll be over *Zathus* after lunch," the Nari scientist said as he entered. "We still planning to head down to the surface?"

Marc gestured the man to take a seat. The office was small for a Vanir, almost cramped, since Cinnra had been almost two feet shorter, but it worked for both Warreth and Nari.

"No offense to you and the girls, Zorge," Marc began. "But with Gonquah taken down, I only have four androids now, and likely we'll never be able to get more, or even possibly fix these if something happens to them. It's time I brought in some serious firepower."

"We're really going to build a new wormhole station?" Zorge asked. "The prices for everything went through the roof after the Constables cracked down. Under the table, it's even worse."

"That's why we kidnapped Elgannohn Shevskara," Marc said. "And took his cute, little daughter, Arieala. I'm just glad the girl saw the whole thing as an adventure, although I would have never marked you as the paternal type."

"I have grandkits about that same age," the Nari scientist said. "Probably never see them again, but I do know how to have tea with youngsters and read them to bed. What would have happened had the wife called the cops?"

"She would have still gotten the girl back," Marc's face turned hard. "Unharmed. Never doubt that. All the pain would have been the father's to bear. But I'm glad that she listened to reason. And it's not like any of that money actually belonged to Shevskara. He skimmed it off others."

"We're likely to burn through all of it, just buying the gear we need and paying bribes to keep it quiet," Zorge's muzzle ruffled sideways in thought. His whiskers were back, but his ears were merely sideways.

"I can always take more hostages," Marc smiled coldly. "That's almost a bottomless well, when dealing with the kind of element that worked as middlemen. Bent, but only guilty of civil infractions, at the end of the day. The kind of people who budget for bribes and fines as part of their regular business. Use all of the money we got from Shevskara. I can get you more."

"What about the Constabulary?" Zorge asked. "Grodray's team apparently went through the androids without any hesitation."

"They saw them as machines," Marc said. "I would have. Plus, none of the Ellis devices had a weapon of any kind except themselves except fists. I would have liked to have seen what a hundred of them could have done with disintegrators. But when I have humans on the battlefield, even the Vanir will hesitate."

"You're sure?" the Nari hesitated.

"Their worst nightmares made flesh, Zorge," Marc sneered. "Coming for them. Baker and Grodray might be tough enough to handle it, but your average officer will freeze up, at least long enough that a human who doesn't care will be able to shoot them."

"Then what?" Zorge asked.

"Then we shatter the Constabulary," Marc growled heavily. "Sticks and carrots, but I'm willing to unleash the most nightmarish scenarios the *Accord* could possibly imagine. Maybe even worse, since they dream too small to truly encompass what I could really do when I'm angry. We'll bring the Constabulary down. After that, there will always be politicians who would rather kiss the ring than die for their principles. We'll use those to control the rest. That and fear."

"And those of us who aren't human?" Zorge asked. "Where does that leave us?"

"You three, and a few others, are the only people I trust," Marc said. "The humans I'm bringing over are killers, just like me. And they'll turn on me in an instant if they thought they could take over. You along with Maiair and Yooyar, will be the key advisors running things. I know what would bind the girls to the throne. What does Zorge desire most?"

"Me?" the Nari asked.

"You," Marc said. "If you have a vested interest in the future, you'll support it. What is that thing that brings you permanently on board?"

Marc was impressed with the way the Nari sat, deep in thought for several minutes. As far as Marc knew, just being able to run his spy networks and tinker in his labs was usually enough for Zorge, but Marc planned to live forever, once they could figure out the genetic engineering necessary.

He would need this Nari scientist/spymaster for decades.

"I've never really thought down those lines before," Zorge finally admitted. "I'll have to get back to you. What do the girls want?"

"Their own form of immortality," Marc said. "I'll need you to find me some geneticists on a par with Morty and Xiomber. And maybe Liamssen, since all three are now working for the Constabulary and I wouldn't trust them, even if they got rescued."

"That will be a rather tricky ask, boss," Zorge said. "Those three were among the very best on the market."

"You've got years, not days," Marc assured him. "I will bind Maiair to my reign by finding a way to use my genes to give her a son. Our son, who would then be part of the new ruling class I will institute when I turn the *Accord of Souls* into a proper, galactic Empire."

"Good to see you aren't planning small," Zorge grinned at him.

"I will live as long as science can manage it, Zorge," Marc said. "Maybe forever. Humans will break the *Accord* for me, but only so far as I will have a permanent underclass of serfs, unable to rise up and stop me. Those same humans will not be given the sorts of advanced modifications capable of making them a threat to me, so they can compete with those rulers from *Accord* species who had been broken free of the Chaa's conditioning, which can be done. It was already cracking when Cinnra brought me over. I will finish the job."

"Okay," Zorge said simply. "I will put that in the back of my mind while I go about building a new wormhole station. As you said, we've got years. At least, assuming we can stay ahead of the Constables."

"There are only three of them I worry about, Zorge," Marc said. "Grodray and Baker will be easy enough to take down, when the time comes. Then we'll go after Dankworth. Not even a Star Dragon will stop me."

COP

SHE KNEW she should have been happy with the current situation. Thrilled beyond measure at what she had achieved, but Eveth Baker was never one to rest on her laurels. This glass was still half empty. She looked around her impersonal flat and considered the space beyond these tiny walls.

Marc Sarzynski, the criminal mastermind known as Maximus, was out there, somewhere, along with a small core of hard, dangerous killers. And possibly one or more of Gonquah's killer android devices. Chaa alone knew what kind of trouble he might cause with that before they caught him.

But she and the Constabulary had managed to break yet another criminal enterprise. Better, one with extensive notes on delivery addresses and bank accounts. She might yet live to see the *Accord* put back on stable ground, after she and Grodray had been shocked to discover how rotten the foundation really was.

But for Gareth, everything might have fallen by now.

She checked the clock on the mantle. Early in the morning still, but she had already been up for two hours, working out and then reading a stack of reports. It was hard letting go of some of these cases, but she knew that Grodray and his bosses had a different mission for her.

The flat's system chimed with an incoming call.

"Answer," Eveth called out, sitting still on the couch and just breathing. Good meditation to get her day started. Wondering who might be calling this early. "Hello?"

"Morning, Eve," Jackeith Grodray said. "Figured you'd be awake, but thought I'd call instead of knocking too early on the one morning you decided to sleep in."

"I'm up," she smiled.

Sleeping in was something a Constabulary counsellor had suggested she try at least once each week. She had managed it twice in the last three months, but that was probably still more than the previous ten years.

"You had breakfast yet?" Grodray continued.

"I have not," she thought out loud. "Worked out, then read. Been sitting here for the last ten minutes waiting for you to call. Or someone."

"Good," she could hear the smile in the tall man's voice. "I'll be over in a few minutes and we'll get some food. Busy day ahead."

"What's up?" she asked, intrigued by the almost-playful tone. This was a man who was forever serious.

"You'll see," he said cryptically, cutting the signal.

Eveth stood and checked her uniform. The same, blue bodysuit she always wore, with an equipment belt about her flared hips and a thigh holster that was supposed to be more or less covered by a jacket she rarely wore.

Because Grodray had sounded serious, she went back into the bedroom and retrieved her jacket, putting it on and securing the first two buttons at the bottom. Enough to look formal, but still let her move quickly.

Her brown hair was getting long enough that she would either have to get it cut soon, or let it grow long enough to pull back. She hadn't decided which, and had been so busy over the last few months that most personal things had fallen by the wayside. A quick blow upwards was still enough to get it out of her eyes for now.

Jack was up to something. You had to know the man to see the humorous layer underneath that serious exterior. So she waited in the salon until a knock at the door.

Eveth opened it and smiled at her partner. Former partner, maybe. It was hard to tell. They had been paired together by her bosses to give an upcoming, Level-3 Constable like her a Senior Constable to learn from. And have him rein her in some, if that was possible.

Except that Jackeith Grodray was really a Level-7. A Prime Investigator in disguise, able to pursue any crime, anywhere. The free agents of the Constabulary. That thing that she wanted for herself.

Eveth kept telling herself that the bosses, all the way up to the First Inspector, must be impressed with the cases she had helped break open, working with Grodray and Gareth Dankworth, the Star Dragon. They hadn't returned her to regular duty on *Orgoth Vortai.*

She had never planned to save the *Accord of Souls.* She was just a cop, not a messiah. But then, she had never expected it to be so fragile.

"Good," Grodray said as he eyed her. "Was going to suggest you look a little more formal today, if you weren't."

"Oh?" she asked, but he just grinned and stepped back, gesturing her to come with him.

Downstairs, there was a Constabulary private car waiting, rather than an auto-taxi. Something was up, but the man was mum.

At least the first stop was her favorite restaurant for breakfast. It wasn't crowded yet, but *Orgoth Vortai*'s sun was only just coming up over Londra's horizon, so most people were only now stirring. Or settling, as the situation demanded.

"Order heavy," Grodray suggested as the waitress delivered coffee. He proceeded to do exactly that, so Eveth followed suit.

Sounded like one of those days where they'd be in one meeting after another, with no time to eat until after sunset.

"Anything you are willing to tell me?" she finally asked when they were alone.

"Things are about to get more serious, Baker," he smiled grimly, but still with a twinkle in his eyes. "Nothing you can't handle, but a lot of levers had to move first, to get us to today. Now we'll see motion, where everything had been in a holding pattern for the last month or so."

"What about Gareth?" she asked.

Technically, Grodray wasn't her partner anymore, as she was now in charge of bringing the former-human on board, but the man was laid up in the hospital for a bit yet, even with everything that medicine could do.

His injuries fighting the androids might have killed anyone else. Even the Star Dragon had come close to dying, protecting her.

"He'll have a place in what's coming," Grodray nodded. "But there are folks at the top who still distrust him, in spite of everything that man has done for us. You and I will be driving. And it starts today."

She couldn't get anything else out of the man except cryptic smiles as he ate more food in one sitting than she had ever seen. Eveth took that as a sign and did the same, until she was so full she felt bloated.

Outside, the same car dropped them at the local tube station, where they rode to orbit in a different private vehicle and docked on a Constabulary transport rather than a civilian one. As soon as they docked, the transport dropped through a tube, which suggested that the vehicle had been waiting specifically for them to arrive, rather than following any sort of a commercial schedule.

Eveth knew she was home as soon as she looked out the porthole on the far side of the tube. There was something about *Almar* that she could identify just from seeing its disk from orbit.

So, whatever was happening was going back to the beginning. On the world usually know as the *Axis of Time*. Home of the *Accord* government, but more importantly, the home of the Constabulary and the legendary home of the Vanir themselves, when they descended from the Chaa.

The next tube ride dropped them out over Prime itself, the capital city of the planet and the *Accord*. It wasn't as artistically decorated as *Orgoth Vortai*, but then the Vanir who made up most of the population didn't do representative art as compulsively as the Grace did. Plus, the Vanir were the only ones who had the *Chaa* inside them, as children of those very gods who had created everything before Ascending in turn.

But it felt good to come home. Like discarding an old robe to step into a new one, just the sun in the sky seemed to wash Eveth clean.

She kept her mouth shut, though. Baker knew she would never live it down with her mates if they thought she was somehow less that solid granite all the way through emotionally. None of them needed to know that she did hear music in her mind. Stopped to smell the roses occasionally.

Granted, far more today than even a year ago, but she could chalk that up to somehow growing up. Or at least growing into herself.

The vehicle deposited them atop the Axis building, built on the very ground where, according to the Founding Legends, the *Chaa* beings known as *The Communion* had last stood, the most powerful of the new gods, before departing forever in their quest.

Landing on the roof was as serious a signal to Eveth as anything she had ever seen. Everyone else was supposed to land in the vast parking lot and front lawn, before entering the building through the grand foyer that contained an ongoing history of the *Accord*.

It didn't yet have a Star Dragon etched into the walls, but it might, one of these days.

Eveth followed Jack to a drop tube and fell quickly into the depths of the building, holding her breath in more ways than one. Below, Grodray led her through a series of hallways and secured doors until they ended up in a small conference room, somewhere in the interior of the building without any windows.

"Now what?" Eveth asked as Grodray sat and she joined him.

"Now we wait," he said, looking as relaxed as she had ever remembered seeing him.

The wait wasn't long. A door opened and several people filed in, standing at one end of the room and smiling at her.

Eveth was mildly shocked at the company, though. Several Prime Inspectors she had met at one time or another, including Doctor Dalton Fitzroy. In addition, several Command Inspectors and even a few Planetary Inspectors, Level-8's and 9's.

Grodray stood, so Eveth did as well, only then seeing the First Inspector herself, Madam Anen Wardson, somewhat obscured by the others.

Eveth tried to remember to breathe. Especially as the First Inspector smiled and stepped close to greet her, her hands behind her back.

"Eveth Baker," the woman smiled. "It isn't often I get to do this anymore, but I pulled rank here, in spite of tradition."

"Ma'am?" Eveth managed, somewhat at a loss.

It didn't help that Grodray was suddenly grinning from ear to ear. As were the others.

"Traditionally, Jack Grodray would be the one to

do this, Constable Baker," the First Inspector continued.

She pulled out a flat box, perhaps twenty centimeters tall and twelve wide, but only two thick. Flipping it open on a hinge at the top, there was a Constabulary badge resting on a gold, silk cloth. Except this one wasn't cerulean blue like the one over Eveth's heart.

Instead, it was a simple, brass one, a ring about seven centimeters across with the outer band being about half a centimeter wide. Seventeen stars had been etched into the metal, three crossing lines each other to form a six-pointed shape, filled in with something black.

Eveth's breath caught ragged.

"Constable Eveth Baker, it gives me great pleasure to raise you to the rank of Prime Investigator," Wardson pronounced in a warm voice. "Welcome to the College."

The College. The organization composed only of Prime Investigators. The single most elite club in the galaxy, as far as she knew, because you had to be accepted by a group of people who had already proven themselves to be the very best cops there were.

Anen Wardson surprised Eveth even more by kissing her on the cheek after handing her the new badge in its case. Others followed suit, including Grodray.

By the time she had recovered her wits, there was a cake in the middle of the table and glasses of wine or juice.

The big breakfast made sense now. There would

be a party later, and she might not have a chance to eat anything nutritious for a while.

Grodray had a smile where butter wouldn't melt in his mouth.

"You're evil," she accused him.

"Guilty as charged," he grinned back. "But you earned this. And did it more than a year ahead of where the rest of them had expected, so I get to collect on a number of bets along the way."

Grodray had bet on her making it earlier than anyone else?

Huh.

"So now what?" she asked as someone handed her a glass of red wine.

"Today we celebrate," he smiled warmly. "Tomorrow, we're going hunting."

LAST TRAVELER

LAST TRAVELER and the rest of the *Ascended Chaa* referred to the Vanir as *Those Left Behind*. Once, they had all been one people, until *First Immortal* had found the way to *Ascend*. Many others had followed once the way was known.

The others, the vast bulk of their kind, had chosen a corporeal existence instead, one that would eventually result in physical death. The twelve greatest of the *Ascended Chaa* had transformed that remainder into the Vanir and uplifted the other species to keep them company.

The gods all had personal names, but none of them thought of themselves in those terms, it having been so long since they existed as embodied beings. The others frequently referred to him simply as *Last Traveler*, as he was the final one of the *Communion*, the pantheon the Vanir and others called the Great Gods, to cast loose the bonds of flesh.

Even him *was* something a misnomer, as the Chaa had, by the very end, been able to take on nearly any form as their need or fancy required. But he had been of the male gender at birth, some sixteen Chitra ago, one hundred and sixty thousand years as the *Accord* measured such things. and still used such a pronoun internally much of the time.

As the last, he had also had perhaps the greatest sentiment and affection for the others, and volunteered to stay behind for a time to watch over the *Accord of Souls* as it found its place. *First Immortal* had already departed in her haste, as had *Seeker for the Knee of God.*

Docent, also known as *Great Teacher,* and *Magistrate* had taken the new thing, the *Accord of Souls* created by *Uplifter,* and given it knowledge and laws. It had been a magnificent thing to behold, both the departure of his kin as well as the dawning dreams of *Those Left Behind.*

Glory in Sunrise had led the final group, standing on the powerful shoulders of the one known only as *Mountain,* as they cast themselves into the great depths to seek the signposts left by the Creator of the universe. *Last Traveler* had waited nearly a third of a Chitra, more than three thousand years, before he leapt outward to join the quest, always yet keeping a tender spot in his soul for *Those Left Behind.*

For more than four Chitra, forty-seven thousand years, give or take, he had wandered, speaking occasionally with others as he encountered them, updating *Narrator of History* with his tales and sights. Always seeking evidence of God's Great Plan.

Time had brought him back to the tiny island of life from whence the Chaa had once departed, one galaxy among innumerable others in just this phase of the multiverse. He paused to look in on his far-removed descendants. So much had changed, and so little.

The chain of lights still crossed the galaxy back and forth, leaving only that one, dark corner where *Merciless*, at the behest of the others, had wiped an entire section of the galaxy clean of alien life lest that other species expand their militancy beyond the small cluster of stars that they had conquered before encountering proto-gods.

Last Traveler had argued the case for the others to be somehow preserved, contained, but *The Communion* had decided. It had been so great a decision that in fact all of the *Ascended Chaa* had been consulted for the first time since *First Immortal* opened the way.

Last Traveler turned away from the darkened stars and smelled the life of the *Accord*. It brought him such pleasure. Some things had not changed in five Chitra, but that was by design. The Vanir and the others had been placed in a stasis from which they could live out long and prosperous lives, but they would never be allowed to *Ascend*. *The Communion* would be the last of their kind, because they had already destroyed one sentient race, and had no wish to fight a second war, this time with their own children.

But a new smell caught his mind as he hovered above the ancient home. An eighteenth species was present, when the Great Plan called for no such thing for perhaps another Chitra at the earliest.

Last Traveler strode close to examine this upstart being. There were two of them present, both wearing the outward form of the Vanir, perhaps as camouflage.

The species called itself human.

He leapt across space to the place where the human smell originated. One world, well out to the fringe of the galactic spiral, along one of the lesser spurs not even on an arm. Ten billion humans, currently contained within their single system, *Last Traveler* studied them closely, took in all of human history in a few moments.

The species had been advanced enough for consideration, seven Chitra ago when the *Accord of Souls* was proposed. The vote had been lopsided, but not absolute, as the species was yet too warlike, and would have not fit in with the proposed Vanir, without significant modification.

The last human Chitra, as he studied them, had been one of unrelenting war. Killing on scales that took *Last Traveler*'s breath away. Xenophobic to a degree that staggered the psyche, even though they themselves recognized this and worked to contain the dangerous elements with an organization called *Earth Force*. But still they knew failure, and so *Sky Patrol*, approximating The Constabulary of the *Accord of Souls*.

Worse, *The Great Plan* expected that humans would not have achieved even a space-capable civilization for another Chitra, had they somehow survived the many chokepoints available during the Industrialization Phases.

Last Traveler noted one last thing that left even his heart cold and frozen.

The humans had discovered the very wormhole technology that the Chaa had first used to explore the galaxy in embodied forms in their early days, before later *Ascending* into godhead. The species could break out of their single system and perhaps master the very galaxy that the Chaa had worked so hard to create. And do so in a manner of centuries, if not a single lifetime, taking their frantic and breakneck pace of scientific exploration into account.

He would need to contact the others and perhaps gather them into a single place for the first time since the very beginning. As he leapt outward, *Last Traveler* wondered if the efforts of *Merciless* would be called upon again.

FIRE

IT BURNED WORSE than the first time he had tapped the form. Gareth tried to clench his teeth and keep his snout shut, but the pain was too great to hold back. His bellow echoed back seconds later from the surrounding mountains, but he was mindless with pain to hear it.

Every transformation hurt. It required reshaping his human body, his Vanir form, and forcing it to grow into a giant, winged lizard. The Star Dragon.

Thankfully, the giant landing field where he frequently trained was empty today. Only the usual team on the training base, faces he knew well enough, even as he had been purposefully kept at a distance from them by security needs.

The morning air was crisp enough that Talyarkinash's breath steamed as he had watched her, but no snow had yet fallen. Perhaps in a few days, if the forecast was correct. Gray skies hung low overhead with potential, but nothing as yet fell.

Gareth opened his dragon's eyes and gazed out at

the field around him. The giant Quonset-like huts used as hangars. The tower from which a few live people supervised the systems that brought auto-taxis and such as needed.

It being too cold outside, Morty and Xiomber were up in the tower, wrapped in silly, striped scarves they had acquired somewhere and sipping hot chocolate. Only Talyarkinash was down here with him on the tarmac in a heavy coat.

He gazed down at her now, noting the remains of the casts that had been cut off both of his hands and forearms before he shifted.

"Are you all right?" she asked simply.

She was one of the best geneticists alive, but lately her job was as much psychologist and friend as medical professional.

The Star Dragon flexed his front paws, resting on his haunches with his wings flapping just enough to keep his length upright.

If you could somehow take the burning itch of a bad sunburn and apply it internally, it might feel like this. But that was still ten thousand times better than it had been yesterday.

"Yes, I think," his low voice rumbled back to her.

Gareth always felt like he had a foghorn for a voice in his draconic form. That low, mournful sound calling across the fog-shrouded waters of the Golden Gate at night.

He twisted, this way and that to make sure that there were no kinks or burns left. Those androids, the Ellis devices that Marc had designed, had nearly done him in. Had Senior Constable Grodray and his team been three minutes later, they would have ended up burying Gareth with military honors.

Or whatever it was that the Constabulary did when someone was killed in the line of duty.

Even if he was a renegade human impersonating a Vanir while trying to stop his former best friend from destroying the galaxy.

"Everything looks good from here," she said, stepping sideways for a better view.

"One quick flight, then?" he asked.

She was in charge of his recuperation. And he would listen to the woman.

"A short one, but don't perform any flying stunts today," she replied. "Just up, around a bit, and back."

Rather than reply, Gareth took a running leap and threw himself into the sky, letting his programmed instincts find the thermals to ride, even on a chilly morning like this. It took work to gain altitude, extra energy reserves that he burned prodigiously at a time when he had barely been eating enough to heal himself. Gareth smile to himself and understood why he shouldn't push things, as much as he wanted to.

Up in a spiraling column, until he was five hundred meters in the air and Talyarkinash was merely an ant in the great distance. He nosed over but kept things controlled, rather than the mad dive he liked to do. Here, he merely fell out of the sky like a feather, swooping by the Nari woman at a lazy hundred kilometers per hour, rather than his craziest top speeds.

Just because, he opened his mouth and scorched a section of the reinforced tarmac with a cone of fire, a burst of binary liquid that burst into a ravening belch hot enough to destroy things.

Except Sarzynski had planned for that. Had made the androids tough enough to resist dragonfire.

Gareth would have to go back to outthinking one of the smartest men he knew.

He banked up and over, reversing his line of flight quickly enough. Because he could, Gareth swooped close to Talyarkinash and thrust himself up in the air, stalling with a big backblast of wings over her head, until he could land almost as softly as a cat.

She had a frown on her face. He had been expecting a smile. It got pronounced when she pulled out her pocket scanner device and aimed it at him.

"Could you drop flat and stretch your tail as far as you can?" she said.

It sounded like a question, but Gareth knew better. He complied, happy that his keel scales would protect him from the cold asphalt for a while.

The Nari woman walked down his right side, aiming the scanner at him. She stood still for a moment and then turned and walked back to his snout.

"Interesting," she said absently.

"What?" he asked, maybe just a little nervous.

"According to this, you are close to twenty-eight meters long now, Gareth," she said. "When you had been merely twenty-seven before."

"I'm still growing?" He was a little shocked. "I thought that you and the boys had set that."

"We did," she was still staring at the scanner's readouts. "You seem to be doing this yourself."

"Me?"

"We'll need to run more tests," she decided. "Could you change back, please?"

Again, she aimed the device at him. This transformation wasn't nearly as painful, but shifting back to human, Vanir, form never was. And his hands hurt less. Barely at all, or perhaps about as bad as if a nun had smacked him on the wrist with a ruler.

At least the bodysuit she had built for him was warm enough in this form, as long as he got inside in a bit. Or put a jacket on.

Talyarkinash walked close. The scanner beeped and pinged merrily.

"Okay, good," she said, eyes intent on the device. "Your regular form is unchanged. I had feared that you might be turning into a giant of a Vanir as well, but the shift appears to be limited to the Star Dragon."

"What does it mean, though?" he asked.

"I have no idea, but I'll talk to Xiomber and Morty, and perhaps Dalton, and see what they think. For now, you can be cleared for duty."

That was the best news he'd had in almost a week, so Gareth didn't mind the rest. He could get back to stopping Marc.

And saving the galaxy.

THE DESERT

WHILE HE HAD JUST BEEN in Arizona recently enough, it had been years since Royston had gone out into the desert itself, just to explore. Not since… no, best not to even think about that time. Those security clearances would not even be reviewed until at least fifty years after the last of them were dead, just to protect the reputations of everyone involved.

Still, some days, Royston missed being a Field Agent in Earth Force Sky Patrol.

It was morning. The sun was just beginning to rise in a pool of molten, red fire to the east as Royston navigated the vehicle north and west into the high basin. The Nevada Territory had been an American State once, when enough rain fell here to support human life at places like The Meadows. For the last century, it had been a ghost town hundreds of miles across and haunted by the memories of past glory.

He had requisitioned a personnel truck from the motor pool with the orders Alvin had sent along. Comfortable enough for eight to travel, it allowed the three of them space to bring extra gear and still stretch out.

Behind him in the backseat, in front of the only known human wormhole device, the two women had settled in as though old friends. Everyone was still on their personal clocks from The Arsenal, set to London time, so they had not minded catching the restaurant as it wearily opened and then gorging on a heavy breakfast, before driving out into the wilds of the desert.

The vehicle had a solar-absorbing skin to power the batteries, plus a tiny thorium reactor, so they would risk only running out of water, but Royston still had all of his desert skills from the old days, if it came to that. And radios he could use to call for help to drop on them in minutes, were the situation to arise.

"Is there any place better or worse, Ms. Darzi?" Royston called as they made their way along the ancient asphalt hardtop.

"There is not, Dr. Loughty," the Grace woman replied from behind him.

"Please, call me Royston," he said. "My daughter uses Father most of the time, so Dr. Loughty makes me feel too formal, especially with what is hopefully to occur."

"Royston," she seemed to try the name on for size, pausing for a long moment. "In another world, I might have once been known as Ilak Vorta."

"I shall endeavor to remember that," he smiled at her in the rear view mirror. "Especially if we are successful."

"Speaking of success," Pippa spoke up. "Why did we need to bring the machine with us, Father?"

"Much of the internals have not been adequately dismantled and scanned yet, my dear," he smiled at his daughter as well. "The original plans exist, but my mechanical geniuses that built this contraption had to use as much art as engineering to get it to where I needed the machine. Were we gone, Alvin or someone would have inevitably taken it upon themselves to produce a full as-built blueprint, which is the last thing we want. Especially as we know it works. We are buying time."

"I see," Pippa concluded. "And we are not supposedly traveling to England at some point to locate that woman and her band?"

"In time," Royston mused. "I suspect that she will be necessary, somehow, for the next steps, but I could not explain why I feel that way."

"I am intrigued by this rock and roll phenomenon, Dr.—Royston," Darzi said. Or maybe Vorta, but he decided to think of her by her human guise, at least for now. Less chance of making a mistake later. "You found the secrets to the higher mathematics contained in music?"

"I realize how strange that sounds," Royston began, but she cut him off.

"Oh, no, that much is clear, Royston," she said. "The Grace live in a world of such rich sensory experience that we feel constant sympathy for the rest of the galaxy, to live in such a dull, dreary place. I have had to explore it myself recently, with my tentacles so greatly limited."

Royston looked up in the mirror. She had shed the hijab that hid her secret once they left the restaurant, and apparently not taken the drugs that kept her tentacles quiescent this morning. They roiled slowly like a snake ball, tasting and sensing the cool, Arizona air and the rising sun.

"Depending on how the rest of this goes, perhaps we will be able to track down that young woman and enjoy another performance," Royston offered.

"I would like that," the Grace woman replied, a distant, airy smile on her face as she got to fully immerse herself in the desert.

They rode for another hour or so, climbing up into the mountains, from which they would in turn descend into the basin below.

"I think this would be a good place," Royston announced.

Royston slowed as they reached the peak of the road, along a vast shelf looking down a thousand feet or more into the dry wadi below, where a tributary of the mighty Colorado River had once strode forth.

Before the dry times.

He pulled the vehicle to the side of the road and parked it in a place that might have once been a scenic overlook, exiting to enjoy the morning air before it grew unbearably warm. A quick-deploying pavilion would provide them protection from the sun while they waited, and Royston had packed sufficient water and food for a week, if necessary.

"Now what, Fatima?" he asked carefully as they stood together.

"Now I will convey your message to my superiors, Royston," she replied. "I can only estimate what their reply might be, but hopefully they will allow me to return, if only to deliver it myself."

He nodded as the imposter, the Grace woman stepped back. Royston felt Pippa take his arm and they watched the other being activate a device disguised as a simple wrist watch.

From his jacket pocket, Royston heard an insistent beeping.

He had forgotten he carried the little alarm with him, but it was apparently detecting the first traces of a new wormhole coming open, so his theory and construction had been on the beam.

Royston left it beeping. He was too fascinated watching the golden haze that suddenly seemed to appear around the Grace agent, Ilak Vorta, sometimes known by some as Fatima Darzi. She smiled once, and then disappeared, fading rather like morning dew subject to golden sunlight.

"Now what, Father?" Pippa asked, once they were alone again.

"Now we wait," Royston said. "And perhaps, dear daughter, we should pray."

SHOPPING

"HOW DID IT GO?" Marc asked as Zorge slipped into the penthouse suite's office, having made it past several people with guns arrayed in layers around him, from the ground floor entrance to the outer chamber of the suite itself, to the door with the first android guarding.

"Clock's ticking, but we've got time," the Nari spymaster replied, throwing himself wearily into a chair.

Marc paused what he was reading to study the man. The fur around the muttonchop whispers was coming in more gray now than it had even a few months ago, as with the longer locks on top. Marc forgot how old the man was, because he himself hadn't yet made it to thirty, but the big, cuddly killer kitty was over fifty by some amount. In the last third of his lifetime, at least. The notes on his age were just estimates, plus known dates of what the man had been involved in, in his youth.

"What did they say when you arrived?" Marc asked.

"And I quote: *Crap, you're not dead?* Unquote," Zorge laughed lightly. "Your reputation will carry them long enough to get the job done, but we'll need to take all our parts and run away with them afterwards, rather than trying to build a new facility here."

"They've lost their fear of me?" Marc scowled.

It had been barely a year since the Constables had broken Marc's hold on the underground of *Zathus*.

"Oh, that's graven into their souls at this point," Zorge replied. "Damabiath's death guaranteed that. Someone will overcome their terror at some point and whisper to a cop, and there are very few bent ones left on this planet. They'll be afraid that they're going to be next."

"Understood," Marc said simply. "I miscalculated. On *Earth*, that would have been sufficient, but the equations are different here. Plus, we look like we're losing right now, and morale, as they ancient Marshal once said, is three to one to the material."

"Meaning?" Zorge's eyebrows came down in apparent confusion.

"Momentum favors the Constabulary over the recent few months," Marc said. "So people want to be on the winning side, rather than digging in for the long term. Once we start winning again, all those people will come out of the woodwork again to explain how they were always supporting you, but had to make it look good to the authorities."

"Gotcha," Zorge leaned back. "We have untraceable cash in hand, and fear, so they'll provide us everything. The first double-cross will probably come when they arrange delivery."

"Assuredly," Marc agreed. "Keep watch on the delivery systems as much as you can. I'd be fine with us hitting a postal truck in route with our equipment aboard. We can pay up later, plus they'll be able to collect the insurance."

"And that won't piss them off?" Zorge's confusion was back.

Truly, the *Accord* confused Marc at times. Even simple things like casual violence seemed to be alien to their nature. And Zorge was broken, compared to the rest of them.

"I don't care," Marc growled sharply. "Once we have everything built and working, nobody will dare speak a word askance. Do we have estimates on timelines?"

"Some of it was already in hand, but I didn't make delivery arrangements, because like I said, I think we need to load it on a truck and then fly the truck straight to orbit and disappear."

"I agree," Marc nodded. "When the transport comes around again, time everything that needs to be picked up so we can do just that. Especially if we can hijack the rest in transit."

Something on Zorge's face caught Marc's attention.

"Second thoughts?" Marc asked.

"Thinking about the future," Zorge admitted. "About that place where you've won and have taken over the *Accord* and turned it into…what's the human word again?"

"Empire," Marc filled in.

"Yes, Empire," Zorge agreed.

"And?"

"And I'm feeling old and worn out today," Zorge said. "Can't find that thing that would break me out of this rut and ground me hard in your Empire, even though I know it should be there."

"Did you want to simply retire at that point?" Marc asked. "Be set up with a lab to tinker and a budget to play? Go fishing? I need you. Your brilliance. Your conniving. Your connections. You are an integral part of this future."

"I understand," Zorge said. "I think I'm an introvert and need time away from people to recover, and we've been on the run for a year."

"Two more months, and you can have all the time you want, Zorge," Marc promised him. "Just give me two months to get us all there."

"That I can do," the Nari sighed, falling in on himself for a few seconds. "Anything else you needed for now?"

"No," Marc said. "We'll need to plan some raids to steal some things legitimately, but nothing that needs to happen today. Can you send Maiair in when you go out?"

"Will do," Zorge said as he withdrew.

Marc sat and contemplated things. He had seen older conmen go through that phase, when they thought they had seen it all and done it all, and just didn't have the fire in the belly anymore.

"You needed me?" Maiair asked as she stepped in.

Like her Warreth sister Yooyar, Maiair's feathers were primarily crimson, with black and white secondary feathers around the edges. Her headcrest was at half-mast today, which he had expected, and her short beak was partly open.

"Sit," he gestured to the chair Zorge had just vacated. "We need to talk about Zorge."

She bristled and Marc caught a motion to her pistol, but it was only a twinge.

"What's he done?" she demanded.

Maiair was his Chief of Staff. The smartest person in the gang after him. Her younger sister was the second deadliest, but Maiair was no slouch in that category.

"He's feeling depressed," Marc said simply. "So we need to find him a smart, cunning, abjectly-criminal, young Nari woman who will play to his ego and experience."

"A bimbo?" she asked, almost angrily.

"No more than you or your sister are," Marc snapped. "He's been an outlaw too long, and now that endgame is approaching, he's rethinking about all the choices that have alienated him from his family in pursuit of power. That much, I understand. I want him re-energized. If he considered crossing-species, I would ask one of you to find me a cousin with the same fire in the soul as you two have, but it will have to be Nari. Perhaps, Grace, if we could find a psychologist in our ranks who could help him over this hump while being beautiful."

"Oh," she seemed chagrined, but confined herself to that one syllable.

"And while I'm thinking about it, we'll need to consider my needs as well," Marc said carefully. Her headcrest semaphored up, just a little. Not much, but he was paying attention. "I will need to locate an appropriate Second Wife when we are finally able to return to Earth."

"Second wife?" she repeated, confused.

Marc smiled at her. It was time to go beyond the occasional moments of pleasure they had stolen in the past year.

"You are, and always will be my First Wife, Maiair," he said, as tenderly as he could. "The second wife will be for the good of the Empire we will forge. And future generations."

"Oh," she said quietly, her headcrest collapsing as the shock hit home.

Marc let her stew for a few moments.

"What will she be like?" Maiair asked in a tiny voice.

Marc leaned back and considered. At one point, Philippa Loughty had been his perfect choice. Beautiful, intelligent, lively. But she had chosen the heroic one, as he had somehow always known she would.

It didn't still hurt any less, six years later.

"Tall and athletic," Marc said carefully, envisioning her in his mind. "Beautiful and erudite. A first-rate, scientific mind, but one not constrained by the sorts of antique morality that would prevent her from participating in our mission."

"A human version of Talyarkinash Liamssen, then?" Maiair asked.

Marc was gobsmacked. Yes, exactly her.

He even knew a few such women, back home, against which he could compare, rather than using Loughty as a benchmark. They would probably still be stewing that they could not be allowed into the refined heights of the sciences.

"Yes," Marc agreed. "Although we may need to kidnap our target, since I can't just walk into her life as a Vanir and expect a rational response."

"I remember you as human, Maximus," Maiair said. "Vanir is just an improvement, but I see no reason that would stop any smart woman."

Marc fixed his future First Wife with a hard eye, but could detect no conniving in her. Perhaps she was sincere. Time would tell, especially when there was a second generation of the ruling caste, chafing at the bit for power, and thrust against one another.

He just needed to get them there.

A CLUE

AT LEAST NOTHING had changed about their outward relationship. Eveth was still a mere Constable, as far as most people were concerned. At least in public. Jackeith was a Senior Constable. The two of them were partners investigating crime.

It was only in her secret heart that they were now both Prime Investigators, Level-7's, and tasked by the First Inspector herself to see this thing through.

She looked around the back of the large vehicle, flying across the afternoon skies of *Irron* on the way to the tube station. Grodray was reading something on his tablet device. Gareth and Dr. Liamssen were whispering like siblings, facing her. Xiomber was asleep, snoring ever so quietly.

"So why *Zathus*?" Morty asked quietly, turning and looking up at her instead of staring out the window.

Eveth considered her possible answers. On the one hand, this man was a hardened criminal with decades of crimes to his name that he had admitted to in court, and was eventually going to be sentenced, once the full scale of problems came out.

On the other hand, he and Xiomber had happily turned state's evidence, putting their eidetic memories for details to paper, including dates, payments, and witnesses to various conversations.

The underworld on *Zathus* had been shattered as a result, like a bug hitting a windshield at high speed.

But his question made sense, as the Constabulary had made such deep and terminal inroads into the various criminal organizations that had grown up slowly, like pearls accreting materials over the many decades.

"Because we missed something," she finally admitted to the little, Yuudixtl scientist. "With what you and your brother provided, we should have been able to round up everything, but Maximus stays ahead of us at each step."

"That's because there are that many bent cops out there, Baker," Morty sneered at her. "Them I can't name, because I never dealt directly with most of them, but the organization had massive inroads everywhere. You cleaned your own house out yet?"

Eveth blushed, in spite of her anger and her effort to suppress it. Gareth and Liamssen had fallen silent, watching, as had Grodray. Xiomber still snored.

"Yeah, thought not," Morty said. "So what can we find on *Zathus* that you missed? Otherwise, you wouldn't need me and Xiomber tagging along."

"What's the next step that Maximus will take?" Eveth replied simply. "That's what nobody has been able to answer. We've been two steps behind him for a year, but no closer than that, or we would have caught him quickly after the birth of the Star Dragon.

He has to be getting help we've missed, so I want to return to where it all started and look again."

She nodded to Gareth, acknowledging their old argument about him sparing Sarzynski's life in trade for hers, Grodray's, and Liamssen. At the time she had been angry, but Jack had gotten her over that, with the expectation everyone had that it was just a matter of time.

"Could he have gone someplace else for help?" Morty asked.

"We've looked everywhere," Eveth snapped at the tiny man.

"No, you haven't," he said grimly. "I know that for a fact."

"Because we haven't found him?" she almost sneered the words

"Because you haven't looked on Earth for one," Morty said, turning to Gareth. "Would he go there?"

"He'd be trapped," Gareth spoke up quickly.

"Not if he had enough equipment to make two stations," Morty said. "Build one and open a wormhole. Chuck everything and everyone through, and then sabotage the machine to eat itself when it's done. Go hide somewhere on Earth and build a new machine, while recruiting people there. The killer robots were a great idea, but you smashed that, so he's got to be getting desperate for help he can rely on. After all, me and Xiomber double-crossed him. What's to stop someone else?"

"Gareth?" Eveth turned to their human expert. "Would that work?"

She noted that even Xiomber was awake now, but the vehicle was utterly silent save for the drives pushing them through the air.

"If he had a generator powerful enough, or plans to build one?" Gareth replied. "Yes. And there are any number of places he could hide, even as a Vanir. Gold is still a medium of currency exchange, so getting enough to buy friends and supplies on Earth would be pitifully easy. And he probably still has friends he could contact."

Eveth turned to Grodray, on her opposite side from Morty, in more ways than one, and caught his silent nod. Yes, they might have to look on Earth as well. What would the First Inspector say?

FIRST INSPECTOR

FATIMA TRIED NOT to grind her teeth as she told the story again.

At least they had taken her seriously, as mad as her story had sounded, even coming out of her own mouth. But Fatima Darzi, the once and future Ilak Vorta, had been nothing if not compelling. And the First Inspector's staff had listened to her. Then escalated things very quickly to the boss herself.

Fatima was inside the woman's inner office within twenty minutes of stepping through that wormhole from Earth. Anen Wardson sat patiently on her couch, while Fatima sat in one of the two chairs.

"Just like that?" the First Inspector asked as Fatima finished her explanation.

"We made mistakes," Fatima said, gesturing to the building around them. "In background research, planning, and execution. Some of them were pure bad luck, but others were failures of context on our part. Those I can help remedy later with new training and documentation, but for now, we are facing perhaps the single most intelligent example of the species currently living. Our one mistake, in selecting Fatima Darzi as the point of access, functionally confirmed what had been mere speculation on his part prior to that. That potentially hostile aliens were behind the disappearances of Dankworth and Sarzynski. Worse, that infiltrators might be coming and they should be on their guard."

"But the knowledge is contained?" Wardson asked.

"Indeed, madam," Fatima replied. "More than contained. Loughty has specifically isolated himself, his daughter, and the one piece of equipment capable of generating the tube. They are far from anyone else in a desert setting, awaiting developments."

"He does know that we could just kill him, correct?" Wardson pursued.

"We did not discuss that scenario explicitly, but I am confident he is aware of it," Fatima said. "I would almost consider this to be an offer of sacrifice on his part. His life, and his daughter's, for the continued existence of humanity. However, he is absolutely convinced that someone would eventually be able to replicate his work, for merely having known that it was possible in the first place. What he is offering us now is time. Without his direct effort, he does not believe that anyone else will be able to replicate the mathematics that currently only existent in his head, for at least another century."

"So the humans cannot be contained," the First Inspector's voice turned harsher.

"Not for long," Fatima agreed. "Once they have the technology understood, it becomes a matter of scale and power for them to reach orbit quickly, and then to their various colonies. After that, they will turn outward and look for other worlds to colonize, unaware how many are so close enough to their needs as to require minimal bioforming. To say nothing of all the worlds of the *Accord* itself, where humans could live easily."

"What have you promised him?" Wardson asked.

"To relay the message to you," Fatima said. "That he did not kill me when he had the opportunity, did not unmask me to anyone else, isolated himself where he could be eliminated with minimal risk to us, all of this speaks towards a desire on his part for some peaceable solution, if one can be found."

"Can one?" Wardson asked. "Is there some outcome that would work?"

"Royston seems to think that Gareth Dankworth would be able to find something," Fatima said. "I have never met the man, nor spoken to any of his handlers, so I have only the perspective from the humans, but the man seemed to have no enemies at all, from what I was able to determine, during my time with the Earth Force people, as well as Sky Patrol. That, hopefully, speaks well of him."

"It does," Wardson agreed. "Especially in light of the methodology originally used by the Yuudixtl criminals to locate Dankworth in the first place."

"Are we at a greater risk if we bring them here, or send a representative there?" Fatima asked. "Working on the assumption that you desire the Loughties to continue alive?"

"They are isolated?" the First Inspector asked.

"Yes," Fatima acknowledged. "But Royston seemed of the opinion that help could be only a short time away, in an emergency, so I would presume that watchers overhead could react to an incident."

"I, as well," Wardson said. She paused for a moment to think. "I will need to take this to the Commission."

The First Inspector rose from the couch and picked up her handset on the desk, dialing and smiling at Fatima.

"Commissioner?" Anen Wardson asked after a moment. "I have a situation that requires your attention, as quickly as you can spare some time."

She paused, eyes distant.

"Now? Yes," she said. "In my office."

She hung up and returned to her spot on the couch, facing Fatima in one of the chairs. Her hands clenched and unclenched in a nervous movement.

Petim Diazal joined them in less than ten minutes. The Commissioner was an Arawath, one of the amphibious species of the *Accord*, looking like miniaturized, blue versions of Vanir. The man was about Fatima's height, slender and rather short even for that species. He dressed sedately, in a charcoal business suit neither too expensive nor too flashy.

But his eyes burned with a charisma and brilliance that made it obvious why he was at the top of the government.

Quickly, the First Inspector related some background, and then Fatima repeated her story for the man.

"It seems utter madness," he said as she finished. "A century to go from this to invading the *Accord*?"

"Human science, from what I have studied, appears to be frequently the result of a lone genius trying something, which can then not be disproven by others, until eventually it becomes canon," Fatima explained. "The genius is the unpredictable element in the whole equation, as stochastic analysis breaks down."

"I do not know how the Commission itself would react," he said to both of them. "At present, I suspect that the tendency would be to overreact. To simply wipe the humans from the face of history defensively."

Fatima cringed.

"And yes, I understand what a significant stain that would be on my soul when I go to meet the Creator," he continued. "Suggestions otherwise?"

"I would like to bring him and his daughter here," the First Inspector said. "We can contain him then. Exile him from the rest, if need be, without necessarily killing him."

"What of the musician?" the Commissioner turned his attention to Fatima. "I do not understand her role in this escapade."

"It is a human concept, Commissioner," Fatima tried to explain. "The genius has a muse, frequently female to his male historically, who inspires him to ever greater heights. It exists in many of their creative arts, and apparently mathematics was close enough for Royston Loughty."

"Then you must accompany Loughty to such a performance before we can remove him from Earth, Constable," he replied in a hard tone. "See what her power is, since we all begin to see that humans have only started to tap their own abilities. Gareth Dankworth is an example of their unknown capabilities, as much as Royston Loughty. If necessary, she may need to be kidnapped and exiled as well."

"Could we hobble the humans that way?" Wardson mused aloud. "Remove their most dangerous elements secretly, that the rest might pose less of a threat?"

"It would not work, First Inspector," Fatima said quietly. "There is an old Irish proverb that covers this among the humans. When asked how many generations it would take to replace them all, if something were to happen to every poet and musician in Ireland, the correct answer is *One*."

"One?" the other two gasped in harmony.

"One generation," Fatima said. "It is, as I understand it, a human thing. And nothing can stop it."

QUEST

THEY HAD CAMPED OVERNIGHT and prepared a pleasant breakfast at sunrise. Royston was enjoying a bowl of tobacco and the last of the pot of coffee, while Pippa sat across the small fire from him and worked her way steadily through Plutarch. Without looking, he guessed it to be around nine in the morning, as the heat was just starting to sand the fine edge of chill off the air.

His pocket began beeping madly, signaling that a portal was about to open. Was in the process of opening near them. Would be here momentarily.

Royston rose to face his fate. Pippa closed her book and did the same. This might be the end of the world, depending on what decision the aliens had made.

An assassin might appear before them. Or a bomb. He would expect the former to be more likely, as they would need to collect the two bodies and then make the vehicle disappear.

Royston would face it unarmed. The pistol was in

the truck, locked safely away against need, none of which rose to this occasion. He clenched the pipe in his teeth and turned in the direction of a metaphorical pull.

Psychic, perhaps. Not something that impacted on the physical senses, but his mind could still place it. They would emerge: *there*.

The air took on that golden hue. A slight breeze seemed to emanate from it, which made sense. A smart alien would want positive pressure, to keep human germs and viruses from somehow leaping across the galaxy to possibly infect innocent and unprepared worlds.

A shape took form as he watched. Briefly, he regretted not having a high-speed scanner camera set up to trigger now, so that he could go back and analyze the event.

Fatima Darzi appeared before them. He could think of her on those terms, as she had replaced her hijab with great fastidiousness, atop the crimson uniform of the Women's Auxiliary. And she was unarmed, so perhaps he would live to see another day.

And perhaps the Lords of the *Accord of Souls* had some hope yet for humanity. Or had simply not gotten far enough along in their planning and execution to finish the species off yet today. Darzi could always be withdrawn at a moment's notice, especially if you had the ability to release bio-bombs all over the Solar System.

Royston held out a hand, which she took in both of hers.

"Good news, perhaps," she offered with a thin smile.

She surprised him by turning and hugging Pippa, who had initiated out of habit.

Royston grabbed a spare chair from where it had been folded up against the side of the vehicle. He gestured them all to sit.

"Tell me," he commanded lightly.

"No decision had been made," she replied. "However, they would like me to visit this musician and evaluate her impact on all of this."

"Her impact?" Pippa asked.

"The First Inspector read me in one some details that I would need, in order to proceed," Fatima said. "Things I had not needed to know prior. Humans, at least as expressed by Gareth Dankworth and Marc Sarzynski, are possessed of a psionic potential that is only rarely tapped, and far in advance of any of our species. In Gareth's case, if provides him the ability to transform into a dragon. My superiors would like to explore the theory that it was only via the combination of Royston's mind and this woman's music that anything could create the psionic gestalt needed to achieve what you have done to date."

"How does that help our cause?" Pippa pressed, concerned.

"If it is such a thing, daughter," Royston interrupted, "then for another to replicate what I have done is a task of such long odds that they may rest easier. It maybe yet be out of humanity's reach to build a large enough device to threaten our neighbors anytime soon. Am I right?"

"You are," Fatima said. "The machine, as you have noted, requires an extraordinary amount of power to do something so simple as move a small glass sphere a matter of meters. Without significant technological breakthroughs, being able to move a man to The Arsenal from the ground here will hopefully be progress measured in centuries, rather than months. Given humanity's evolution over the last thousand years, there is hope that they may yet achieve true civilization in that time."

"Most war and crime is a result of want," Pippa said, bringing her lessons in the social sciences to bear. "Of poverty, both physical and emotional. As Roosevelt once said, freedom from want will lead us to freedom from fear. If we could move past poverty at a global and systemic scale, humans can be fantastically warm and giving people."

"So my superiors hope, Pippa," Fatima replied. "Based on your history, there are bright lights in the darkness that we can pursue."

"I am not the only possible genius that could do the work," Royston said. "The last thousand years of human history have been an astounding collection of small inventions that opened the doors to previously unimaginable things, just because of human propensity to ask *What if?*"

"Exactly, but if you are not a threat to break out of your home system in the next decade, the Commission does not need to panic and overreact in consequence today," Fatima said. "We can try to find another way."

"There are many who might welcome the *Accord of Souls* meddling in human culture," Pippa noted. "Moreso than you have. Perhaps more publicly, if you will."

"Yes, indeed, daughter," Royston nodded. "But there are others who would object strenuously. Demagogues forever threaten, and it would not take much to rouse a mob at the possibility that intelligent aliens are out there. Then you have the very war we are trying to prevent. Thus the tightrope we must walk."

"Could Earth Force be strengthened?" Pippa asked, more rhetorically than with any seriousness. "Would that help or hinder our cause?"

Royston noted that Fatima sat silently, observing and probably preparing a report based on this conversation. As she should.

"It probably harms us, at least in the short term," Royston mused, letting his mind wander over the things Earth Force was created to prevent, such as wars, and how Sky Force might be twisted by a charismatic, amoral charlatan. "What was fascism, the worst of the Twentieth Century ideologies, but the pursuit of power for the sake of power itself, rather than the betterment of humanity? Better that we shatter the edifice and allow a war that grinds us back down to the iron age, than we turn outwards and conquer a defenseless galaxy."

Pippa shuddered, but made no argument. Pain for a few billion humans, stacked against the deaths of how many trillions of intelligent beings? Royston had no expectations that the better angels of humanity would prevail, at least at first. And how the *Accord*'s psionic harmony might react to a human invasion was something he could happily go to his grave without knowing.

The air seemed to have recovered that chill it had as the sun first rose, but there was nothing to do about it, except soldier on.

"I think it would serve us best if our trip across the badlands of the Nevada Territory was now cut somewhat short," Royston decided aloud. "England would, I believe, be a better choice at present, as long as we are careful."

"What would be the problem with home, father?" Pippa asked.

"I fear what devilment Sir Westfield might get up to, were he to discover we were close," Royston stated. "Unless you think a visit to Buckingham might aid our quest."

He rather liked the way Pippa's face turned to alabaster. Fatima's brows knit together in concern.

"Buckingham Palace," Royston smiled at the other woman. "The home of the Queen of England and her family. Sir Westfield, who was one of my mentors, remains one of her favorites, and the Queen has taken a keen interest in my recent studies. If our presence became known, we may not be able to escape a meeting, yourself most likely included. Given the sensitivities of the subject, I would rather forebear, at least this once."

He rose and began packing things up as the women processed the future. The fire was easy enough to smother with dirt. The pavilion undid itself with a simple button, converting down to a portable unit not much larger than a lunch box. The women quickly joined him in organizing things into the rear of the truck, as he and Pippa had put everything away after sleeping inside last night.

"Now would be a nice time to be able to just step onto a disk and emerge in London," Royston laughed as the truck slowly began to descend the mountains, turned around and headed toward the Gulf Coast again, eventually. "But those are the sorts of labor-saving inventions that might make things worse, so I will simply endeavor to drive us to a spot where the auto-controller unit might take over. Or not. Suffice it to say, we can be in London in a week, if we were to drive to someplace like Boston at a leisurely pace and then catch a flight."

"Perhaps we should not necessarily stop and smell the roses this time, Father?" Pippa noted from the rear.

"Yes, indeed," Royston sighed. "Our destiny awaits us in Merry Old England, I fear. Avoiding it will save us nothing."

Eat, drink, and be merry, indeed, as the ancient saying went. Tomorrow we may all indeed die.

ZATHUS

TECHNICALLY, Gareth had been on *Zathus*, according to Xiomber, but had only passed through the system for the briefest of instants, before being further shunted off into a second tube, to land on *Orgoth Vortai*, where the adventure truly began.

The sky overhead was a little too purple for Gareth as they emerged from the transport. The truck had dropped them at a new Constabulary facility, a small training base just outside the city limits of Seani that reminded Gareth of the ancient National Guard Armories that many states back home still maintained, mostly as vehicle depots for emergencies.

Tall, cyclone fence around the grounds. Red brick buildings two and three stories tall. A garage off to one side that was nothing but closed bay doors right now, with a gravel quad in front and grass over to one side.

Constabulary officers were coming and going as the group organized themselves in front of one of the smaller buildings, but nobody paid much attention, even when only three of the six wore uniforms. Morty and Xiomber had successfully pled their cases to be allowed out in their comfortable, blue dungarees and black t-shirts, although Morty's had a phrase across the front that was right on the borderline of rude and profane, even if it was apparently the name of a musical band.

Talyarkinash wore dark gray: pants, chemise, tunic, and light jacket in various shades and fabrics that flowed together well.

Grodray led them into the building at a pace that left the shorter half of the party almost jogging to keep up, but he wasn't doing it out of spite. Grodray was just like that when he got focused. Inside, the building was apparently unused, at least for now. Gareth was at once reminded of an armory barracks, empty most of the time, with things in storage except for the regular musters once a month and the big training formation annually.

The inside was a big, open bullpen filled with desks, rather like a Constabulary office where Constables and other detectives would work. Forty people could be active in here at any given time, without being too crowded, assuming that one of the other buildings had a canteen running, or you had access to a vehicle to take you to a nearby donut shop.

They were utterly alone in here.

"I have made arrangements for us to bunk upstairs," Grodray announced to the group. "We'll mess with the training cadres over in the main building, which include civilians, so not being in uniform should not present any difficulties. If you feel the need for morning or evening calisthenics, feel free to join the groups in the quad. Eve, I would appreciate if you kept your morning runs inside the fence, just running laps for now. The neighborhoods around here are lower middle class, for the most part, but I expect eyes and ears on the street. They can watch you from over there, but not hassle you personally without inviting more trouble than they ever dreamed possible."

The way he said that last left goosebumps on Gareth's arms. He had seen Baker angry a time or three, but Grodray was always the calm, intellectual type. Rather like Royston Loughty in that, although more of a hands-on type than the scientist back home.

Gareth angrily suppressed the flinch that wanted to shiver through his body. Pippa would be better off without him, if he could somehow convince them he was dead. She might not like it, but she would find a way to move on and have a life, rather than just hanging on forever.

"Dankworth?" Grodray asked.

Apparently, he had detected something.

Gareth shook his head and remained silent.

"Okay, then upstairs and pick out your rooms from the officer's area," Grodray said.

Gareth found all their clothing had apparently been packed and sent ahead, as there were footlockers with names on them in the waiting area at the top of the stairs. Quickly enough, everyone had rooms, with him third down, past Grodray and then Baker, followed by Talyarkinash and then the boys beyond a short gap.

They met up back in the upstairs area, which was

filled on one side with empty triple bunks that were human sized, and the other was a lounge area where you could read or watch videos on a personal device. The majority of the population on *Zathus* was Warreth and Nari, with significant populations of Ramasayia and Enjev, so the human scale made sense, but at least his room was Vanir-sized.

"Okay," Grodray gathered them all together. "Dr. Liamssen, you, Xiomber, and Morty will be able to work here without much interruption, as we've brought over as much gear as you had there, and all your notes. Mostly, you'll continue what you were doing before, which was explore what's happening that Gareth's Star Dragon is suddenly bigger, while trying to identify what we might expect from Sarzynski. Baker, Dankworth, and I will be out on the streets."

"Any of my old friends still around?" Morty asked.

"Doubtful," Baker smiled. "We've either arrested everyone on your list, or chased them so deep under a new rock that they can't even find themselves."

"If that's the case, then you really only have two viable options," Xiomber interjected. "Either a second Star Dragon, which I doubt, or another rogue tube station, like we had here before Morty blew it up."

"Why do you doubt a dragon?" Grodray asked.

"Not his type, old Maximus," Xiomber grinned. "Hell, just convincing him to turn into a Vanir was a big enough pain in the tail. He only went along because *One*: he had to hide in plain sight, and *Two*: we made him the biggest, damned Vanir you could imagine. Those killer robots tell me he's not doing anything more to make himself a monster."

"We've cut off his friends here, for the most part," Morty chirped in. "Like I said earlier, I'm thinking you best look for him on Earth at this point."

"We've got all of the *Accord of Souls* to look in as well," Grodray said. "But I agree that he'll get tired of running. That's why we're here. We've got to find him, and stop him from getting to Earth, because if he uplifts their technology to what we have, then he can come back at the head of an army. The First Inspector has already made it clear to several of us that that is something we can never allow. If it gets to that point, they are prepared to take extreme measures."

"How extreme?" Gareth asked quietly.

Grodray nodded at him before speaking.

"As bad as you surmise, Gareth," Grodray said sternly. "They would be prepared to wipe out all humanity instead of allowing them to escape. You would be the last human."

"I'm not human anymore, Senior Constable," Gareth replied. "I am a Vanir now, even if I cannot join the *Accord of Souls* properly. At least, nobody has figured out how yet. And I am a Star Dragon. But I agree, I might have to be the last, if the alternative is a human crusade against the galaxy. As long as I can kill Sarzynski first."

"It may come to that, Gareth," Baker explained simply.

"I've known that for over several years, Eveth," Gareth replied. "Why do you think I've been trying so hard to prevent the rest now?"

THE CHASE

MARC HAD MISSED this part of the job. He was supposed to be in charge these days, and that meant that he sent others out to pull heists, but truly, there was nobody he knew round here with the skill or panache to do this.

Maiair was close. She had a cool head under that crest, as well as a willingness to shoot someone if pushed. Yooyar, on the other hand, would probably just shoot at the first sign of trouble.

Mishalska, the young Nari punk, was turning into a proper soldier these days, training himself harder than anyone else in the gang. It was almost like being back home on the football field. Watching that one kid who had no size or strength trying to compete with bigger, faster, stronger boys for playing time. That kid had had heart beyond anybody, finally getting to play a few meaningless downs at the end of his last game of his senior year, because Coach had never once seen him flag. Every down in every practice was approached like the winning play at the championship game.

Mishalska reminded Marc of that kid.

Zorge was home minding the store, so Marc had only those people with him.

Oh, and one of three remaining androids. Zorge had the other two, guarding the base against surprises, but Marc figured he could manage this possibly alone.

He needed the others because he still needed others. Gonquah had come perilously close to breaking Marc free of needing anyone in the *Accord of Souls*, before Gareth and that woman Constable, Baker, had taken him down.

Fine. You people want to play rough? Watch this.

Marc could have told these fools that the best way to move stolen and illegal parts around was to do it in the middle of the day. In the worst of the rush hour traffic. A time when the beat cop was too busy trying to direct traffic to step in and look closely at a tractor and trailer toodling along, running low on the axles because the equipment in back was too heavy to even move on repulsors.

Doing it in the dead of night, on abandoned back roads was just an invitation for someone to come along with guns and hijack it.

Marc smiled. Beside him, driving the small truck, Maiair smiled back, as if she could read his mind. Certainly, she had the best brain for it of all of them. She would make a good queen, a Grand Duchess of his new Empire.

In back, Mishalska and the android appeared to be competing with one another to be the most silent.

"One," Yooyar's voice came over the comm. "Countdown."

"Two," Marc picked up the device and keyed it. "Acknowledged."

There. Nothing incriminating, unless you were already paranoid and listening on all bands. Plus you would have to recognize the voices that quickly, and understand that the truck had just crossed the first intersection, coming off the highway, where his killer Warreth babe was sitting in another vehicle, a stolen car this time that nobody would notice until tomorrow.

Marc leaned forward just a little and looked down the long straightaway of the road. He had picked it because the road was old and narrow, almost an alley between a tall, brick wall outside an underworked factory on one side, and several new and used vehicle lots on the other.

If it had been Marc, he probably would have been able to break the ambush by jumping a curb and smashing his way through the parked cars, relying on weight and momentum to get him clear enough, fast enough. Noise and alarms here would bring police in a hurry, but they would have picked an innocent to drive.

Just another load that needed to be delivered tonight, officer. Don't know what was in it that made men and women with guns want it.

Or something like that.

There. Headlights as the vehicle rolled to a four-way stop, precisely looked all directions, and then made a right hand turn onto this narrow street.

I have you now.

"Pull forward and set your brake," Marc ordered, loud enough for the two in back to hear.

Maiair engaged the vehicle and drove it out of the little side alley they had chosen, pretty much blocking the lane and turning the road into a cul-de-sac.

"Everyone out now," Marc commanded, opening the door on his side and moving quickly around to the other side of the panel van. Wouldn't do be standing in front of an on-rushing vehicle, especially if anyone in the cab recognized him and decided to collect the bounty tonight.

The truck began to slow as he saw the roadblock. He wasn't going that fast to begin with, but he didn't immediately jam on his brakes and try to back out of the trap.

Pity. Should have.

Yooyar's stolen car rounded the corner and blocked him in. Rather than try to straddle the middle, she turned it diagonally and jumped out. Even from here Marc could see the glint of streetlights off the heavy disintegrator in her hand.

The driver of the big truck finally realized what was going on.

And panicked.

Marc couldn't see the whites of his eyes from here, but he could imagine them. The truck suddenly made a low roaring sound as the driver downshifted the gearbox for power and mashed the accelerator to the floor.

He was going to try to brush the van aside with his mass.

Inwardly, Marc had to give the man credit. He had been expecting an innocent who would roll over politely at this point. He had gotten a soldier apparently willing to push.

Marc drew his own heavy disintegrator and fired a shot past the hood of his van into the ground about midway between the vehicles. The asphalt steamed madly and exploded upward with rubble from the heat, but the driver didn't seem to flinch.

"Shoot the tires?" someone asked. It might have been Yooyar on the radio, he couldn't tell without taking his eyes off the impending avalanche of steel and chrome death.

"Everyone step back from the van," he roared over the sound of the truck closing.

He fired another shot, this time at a transformer box on a power pole. It exploded with a sound like a war, an echo that probably woke up half the town, only to discover that they had lost power.

Sparks flew everywhere, as well as a petite fireball ascending into the night sky.

Marc moved to a spot where he could dive to safety back in the alley where they had parked earlier. He raised his pistol and centered it on the driver's side of the windshield, falling into the classic stance of a Sky Patrol shooter: second hand cupped under the grip. Right foot pulled back behind him for stability. Hunched slightly. Eye, gunsight, and eternity about to pass to the horizon through the cab of the truck. Low, too, just about through the steering wheel, so you couldn't duck and hope.

You'd lose control of the vehicle if you did, at the very moment when it slowed way down from hitting a smaller van. Marc and his people would be able to swarm you, and they would be angry.

Marc doubted stories of human psychic ability.

Nobody had ever been able to demonstrate such things in front of a scientific audience.

At the same time, his posture left no doubt as to his intent, and his willingness to kill at this point. The driver understood.

Inside the cab, the being jammed his brakes to the firewall and pressed the clutch down at the same time. Even that much mass can stop quickly, when you find the will to survive sure death.

The monster rig rolled to a stop less than a foot from the van.

Marc was up on the sideboard with the pistol pointed in quickly, but even as fast as he moved, the Nari driver already had his hands up and face turned to look at his ambushers.

Marc tried the door, found it locked.

"Open this," he snarled, centering the pistol on the man.

The driver reached over very carefully and clicked the lock.

Marc ripped the door open almost as fast as Maiair got the passenger side open.

"I surr-surr-surrender," the driver stammered.

"Out," Marc ordered him. "Mishalska, get in."

Wonder of wonders, the kid had known how to drive a rig like this, so Marc had not needed to recruit or kidnap someone to handle it.

Out on the street, Marc took the man's pocketcomm and smashed the face against a stone wall. That was good enough for now. Disintegrating it would have just been mean, as the man would have lost everything stored on it forever.

This could be fixed in a day.

"Start walking north," Marc ordered, gesturing

the man back the way he came and away from his destination.

The Nari driver looked for the briefest moment like he wanted to argue, before he shrugged silently and started walking.

"Move it, people," Marc called to his team, but they were already moving.

Maiair quickly backed the van into the alley out of the way as her sister and the android climbed in, leaving the stolen car blocking the road behind them. Marc moved to the passenger side of the rig and watched his own Nari driver get it into motion.

Step one complete.

Now Marc just had to build himself a portal, so his new army could come over and show these people how it was really done.

HUNTER

THE SKY in this planet was still too purple, but at least the sun had set. Gareth had long since given up trying to identify constellations in the night sky, since much of the *Accord* was never closer than one thousand light years from *Earth*, but it did bring him some level of peace, just glancing up at the diamonds in the firmament of night.

He was dressed in his favorite cowboy outfit tonight. The place he was going wasn't a rough honky-tonk on the edge of town, where this outfit would go unnoticed, but a more upscale event, where he would draw whispers.

As intended.

He was bait. But even a stalking horse pinned for a tiger can kick, so he wasn't that concerned for his own safety. Besides, he might also be the tiger here. That thought brought a smile to his face as he approached the front gates of the facility, and the two Vanir that had been hired to check tickets.

Gareth had no clue how many such organizations

his cover identity belonged to. With the Constabulary budget involved, he didn't pay any dues, just got tickets to a fund-raiser for some charitable organization from a messenger when he needed to go somewhere. And it was a good cause, so he didn't feel bad as a mole penetrating these echelons of social strata and perhaps spreading his middle-class American values all over the locals.

He was just sorry that Diệu Ahn was unable to join him. He made an even more effective secret agent when she was busy distracting everyone in the room with her competition to show off just a little more skin than was proper, at whatever event she chose to attend. Nobody usually even remembered she had a Plus One, afterwards.

But tonight was a different thing. The time for subtle was past, as the two Vanir men at the front gate inspected his ticket and very politely passed him into the interior. Prime tickets, apparently, at least according to Grodray. Requiring a middle-class manager's monthly salary just to purchase.

Serious money. Just none of it his.

Gareth's grin was irrepressible as he crossed the courtyard and climbed the eight, granite steps to the front door of the mansion. As back home, people with money had a tendency to want to show it off. Thus, a private fund-raiser in the home of some fabulously wealthy philanthropist.

Except this worthy had shown up in Gonquah's records. More than once. The secret records that weren't supposed to exist, suggesting that the man was perhaps not as clean and upright as his public persona appeared.

Elnon Ruaidhrí really did have a gorgeous home.

Almost Georgian, in a place that had no idea who George was or what he might have meant to architecture. White marble exterior with three stories and pillars in front. Windows everywhere. Two long wings of the building reaching each direction from the massive foyer with twin staircases, each covered over with a lush, red carpet.

Perhaps half of the invited guests were already here, mostly in the process of moving from one place to another. Gareth felt a momentary twinge at being so underdressed, with everyone else gone to the nines and gems, but he was a reporter tonight, an outsider supposed to draw glares from the beautiful people.

And his smile could not be helped. He was back in the field, and playing a little game with himself tonight to guess how many of these people were also crooks in disguise.

A few faces he recognized from other parties, mostly with Diệu Ahn, but at this level the circles tended to be small enough. Interestingly, a significant chunk of the guests were Vanir, where he had been one of only a handful, other times.

Gareth passed through the foyer into a grand salon beyond where a side table was filled with finger foods. Wait staff with trays circulated, distributing tall flutes of wine and champagne, although he wasn't sure you could call it that, if it didn't originate in the French countryside. Still, lovely. And ticklish.

The crowd was a little thicker here, perhaps the gravitational center of the party, after all. The host was a Vanir, mostly holding court as Gareth meandered in.

One face jumped out at him as he moved to the fringes of a group studying a portrait of Ruaidhrí's parents over the mantle. Gareth nearly broke cover as his jaw dropped, because he had been expecting her here, just not like *that*.

Eveth Baker had rarely appeared around Gareth in anything more or less than the bodysuit of a Constable. It was a skin-tight outfit that covered her over in armored scales and authority, but she had left it at home tonight.

Instead, she wore a white, silk sheath that clung to every curve and plunged precariously in inviting places. Diệu Ahn would have gone out in such an outfit. Someone had done Baker's hair up, as well as her makeup, so Gareth assumed a professional, as Eveth never did neither herself.

Still: *Wow*.

She caught Gareth staring and grinned for just a moment. Grodray, on her arm, looked every inch the gentleman at leisure, in what Gareth would have classed as herringbone tweeds. Close enough.

"And how are we finding the occasion?" Gareth finally managed to ask, turning beside Baker so as to pretend to stare at the portrait over the mantle.

It was hideous. And he could say that with a professional opinion, given the amount of art he had been required to study and memorize recently. Ruaidhrí's parents looked almost demonic, as though the artist had intentionally overdone the reds and shadows in a way that left their skin almost sallow.

Grodray grunted with something approaching disgust.

"There is a rumor," Baker whispered to Gareth as they stood. "That Elnon took the original portrait and had it retouched later, to reflect his opinion of his sires."

"Do original pictures exist for comparison?" Gareth asked, dipping into his training.

"No one knows," she replied.

"Still, a useful tidbit," Gareth said. "Enjoy your evening."

He bowed to the two of them, as if they were strangers, and departed, seeking other clues and memorizing the layout of things, just in case he ever needed to break in at a later date.

Or just kick in the door with an arrest warrant in hand.

Gareth let the tides of the room draw him slowly around to where his host was standing with a group of people. They were the only two Vanir in this room at the moment, as shorter folks and staff came and went, so Gareth nodded to the man over the heads of a pair of Warreth with jewels in their head-crests.

"You look familiar," Elnon said, obviously trying to place a familiar-enough face.

"*Morthri*," Gareth supplied. "One of Gonquah's rolling parties, if I recall correctly."

He did. Perfectly. Tonight, however, was his role an art critic and reporter who just happened to recognize a face as well, as opposed to having read the man's hefty file, listing all the places where nobody had ever quite gathered enough evidence to put it to a grand jury. Until about a month ago, when Gonquah got arrested.

"Yes, of course," the man nodded. "On the yacht. How silly of me to forget. Enjoying things? Gareth, right?"

"That's right," he replied. "Rather enjoying the art

and architecture. I was mildly surprised when the invite arrived and had your name affixed, as I had no idea you were such a collector. Had I known, I'd have probably been beating down your door long before this."

The two Warreth sensed the change in local environment and made polite excuses to abandon ship, leaving Gareth and Elnon alone for a moment.

"Would you like a grand tour?" Elnon asked. "My wife can handle the crowds for a bit, and this is really more of a meet and greet for the next few hours, at least until the silent auction begins to wind down. Or heat up."

Gareth had noted the collectibles put up for the silent auction tonight and presumed that several of them might bring in a nice annual salary individually, to say nothing of the entire group. This fundraiser would go long ways towards the charity's annual operating budget, all by itself, he gathered.

Pity the man behind it was so crooked.

"That would be lovely," Gareth exclaimed. "Although I might want to come back later with a camera and catch a few interiors and exteriors, just so my editor can put one over on some of the competition. I gather nobody has ever done a full architectural tour before?"

"That's right," Elnon almost preened as he took Gareth's arm in his and directed him to the south wing of the building.

"Truly a shame," Gareth noted as they made their way into a semi-formal library with paintings on the wall and a few sculptures in stone or metal on low pedestals.

Gareth stopped at one painting and cocked his

head slightly.

"Early Eldritch Period?" he hazarded a guess quietly. "It's missing some of the later color and shading elements of the school, but I could see where they grow out of this piece."

"Amazing," Elnon said. "Yes, this was one of the very first transitional pieces when things first moved from the Skybourne School. It has been in the family for almost four centuries, so I'm not sure it has ever been seen in public. How did you know?"

"The Skybourne School always struck me as far too pretentious in their overemphasis on the blues and the use of that damnable, clay paint to add a third dimension to things." Gareth let his mouth sour, just a touch. He really hated that period of *Accord* art. "The Eldritch period reverted to two dimensions, and required the artist to master them well enough to force you to see the third, rather than cheating."

"Well said," Elnon agreed, turning them deeper. "I have a few other pieces in the private wing that should simply unravel you then."

"Lead on, then," Gareth smiled. "I find a sophisticated collector so rare a treat. Too many of them are *nouveau riche* pretenders who hire a buyer and never bother to actually learn about the art underlying."

"This collection has been slowly evolving for a little over five hundred years, my dear man," Elnon's voice got haughty, as expected. He really was old money on this planet. "I have taken it to heights previously undreamt of."

Gareth smiled and let the man lead him deeper into portions of the building no cop had ever seen.

STALKING HORSE

"SO WHAT DO WE KNOW?" Eveth asked as they assembled the next morning.

She was back in her armored bodysuit, feeling more like an professional and less like a bimbo. Undercover work required those sacrifices occasionally, but all she'd had to do last night was watch and study. Gareth, of all people, had managed to play to the target's vanity without them needing her as a pretty face to seduce the man.

But art nerds were a breed apart, and they had already established the Star Dragon with the perfect cover to penetrate that aspect of *Accord* society looking for bad people.

Eveth just wished that crime wasn't such a profitable venture for people. The *Accord* wasn't supposed to be so riddled with corruption. And she would happily take up a second career if they could somehow manage to put all the bad people in jail to the point that the Constabulary was no longer needed to keep the peace.

"Security system is possibly past State of the Art," Grodray replied.

It was just her, him, and Gareth this morning, in a small, private room reserved for a local officer in the unit.

"Past?" she turned and stared at him to clarify.

"I identified a few places where Elnon had installed things I couldn't even identify, let alone defeat," Grodray shrugged. "Not a problem if we just move in an arrest the man. However, trying it represents a problem."

"Correct," Eveth commiserated. "That might trigger Maximus to go underground again."

"Are we sure he's even here?" Gareth asked. "Would he risk staying put if the three of us are poking around?"

"That's what we need to find out," she said. "All the records we retrieved from Gonquah hinted at a connection between Elnon and Maximus, to the point that Elnon was the one that introduced them, but there has been nothing we could use to take him down. His legal team is too good and everything is far enough removed from his person as to make him invisible. Or invincible, as it might be."

"And nobody else had anything better?" Gareth asked.

"It all got burned," Grodray grunted. "Either metaphorically or literally, in a few instances. People panicked and scrammed computers hard enough to eliminate any possibility of recovering data from them. And if you pour water on warm ashes and stir vigorously, you'll get the same effect."

"Well, I agree with you that any paper records the

man keeps will be detailed and meticulous," Gareth opined. "He just had to show off a few of the chains of acquisition around some of the more interesting pieces. Nothing illegal, although he was well beyond ethical behavior to accomplish some of it. But yes, everything is in a nested series of trusts and corporate entities so dense that they might stop a bullet."

"You saw paper records?" Eveth perked up.

"Yes," Gareth explained. "In art, you have to show a complete chain of ownership, all the way back to the original artist, to validate that you have something that is, in fact, not a forgery. That's where most forgers get caught. Copying a painting is relatively easy, but you have to spoof the ownership paperwork, and their professionalism frequently gets the better of them."

"Professionalism?" Grodray asked, eyebrows rising.

"They can't stomach a badly-formatted document, so everything is a little too perfect," Gareth said. "That sets people like me off. Can't tell you how many case files I read where the original, legitimate paperwork showed gaps that were filled in later with initials and dates on the sides, because something passed quickly a few times, and then sat in some dowager aunt's living room for fifty years unrecognized. You have to start a new chain, and then staple it to an incomplete one from the last company that insured a valuable piece."

"Huh," Grodray observed. "You all set to go into art fraud, after we catch Maximus?"

"It was that or a jail cell," Gareth grinned at the

Senior Constable. "Needed to make myself valuable as a Constabulary agent somehow."

"But Art Fraud?"

"Jack, it was your idea," Eveth pointed out. "Use that eidetic memory of his for something useful."

"Well, yeah."

"So he's gotten us in the door a number of places," she concluded before turning to Gareth. "Can you get us inside to maybe crack his personal safe and find the key we need to turn him?"

She liked the way Gareth's face screwed up in concentration. He was a brilliant officer, much of the time, and was taking the time to think right now, rather than just blurting out an answer based on masculine ego.

"You two are too well known to accompany me inside on my next run," Gareth finally replied. "I would assume he'll remember both of you from the party, assuming he ever looked as high as your face, Eveth."

She started to say something tart, but blushed when she saw the smile on Grodray's face. Gareth was at least earnest.

"What will you need?" she asked, rather than sputter at the two men.

Again, serious pause as Gareth broke into the building in his mind, walking through the rooms to the office that apparently had no windows. His hands even pantomimed the process unconsciously.

"There was a dead space," Gareth finally said. "A spot that I can't account for, thinking back and counting steps."

"How big was it?" Grodray leaned forward

almost as quickly as she did. They shared a knowing glance.

"Maybe six or eight feet deep," Gareth mused, eyes unfocused. "Depending on what the walls were made of. It ran between Elnon's bedroom and that office. The closet didn't seem that deep, when I glanced in, compared to the sumptuousness of the bathroom event."

"Event?" Eveth asked, unsure if she had heard the word correctly.

"Event," Gareth confirmed. "Bigger than my current cabin on *Irron* by about double. Makeup counter for his wife. Water closet that really was a closet. Double shower. Oversized, jetted tub that could hold six in a friendly orgy. Gold metal as tiles and plating everywhere, mixed with maroon and blue."

"Panic room?" Grodray asked.

"What's that?" Gareth turned to the older cop.

"If someone breaks in and the owner panics, he can retreat to a small, secured room, armored on all sides, with a separate water and HVAC system and hard-set communications to the outside world, to call for help. They are designed to be proof against anything hand-held, on the logic that you want someone alive."

"I didn't think the *Accord* was into that sort of thing?" Gareth asked, face all confused.

"Criminals almost always turn on each other eventually, Gareth," Eveth noted. "If you had enough money and bad friends, it might be a very useful thing to be able to be able to hide from them while calling the Constables to save you."

"Yeah, but that sounds too defensive," Gareth

squinted at something she couldn't identify. "I'd want my bolt hole to have an escape hatch."

"Why?" it was Grodray's turn to get serious.

"You're in a small box, sure, but now I've trapped you there," Gareth said. "What's to stop me bringing something heavy enough to cut a wall away, if I don't mind smashing the rooms behind whatever beam I cut loose?"

"Tunnel?" Eveth asked.

"We were on the second floor of the North Wing," Gareth's eyes unfocused again and he started counting steps while she held her breath. "Crap."

"What?" she asked.

"There's another dead space on the first floor," Gareth said. "Not far from the Grand Salon. I put it down at the time as a simple pillar stabilizing things, but it's almost exactly under the blank space, maybe six feet across. Ladder down to first floor or maybe the basement?"

"North wing? Just beside the main rest room on the ground floor?" Grodray asked.

"Correct, where the bathroom looked like it had space for a second stall on the left, but the wall juts out at an odd angle."

"What's in the basement?" Eveth asked.

"Garage for his vehicle collection." Gareth started to say. "Crap. Of course. Pop out down below, jump in a car, run like hell."

"Yes, but that means we can get in that way as well," Eveth said. "When you tour the place again, get me pictures we can use for a floorplan diagram."

"Yes, ma'am," he smiled at her.

Eveth finally felt like they were getting somewhere. You didn't need a panic room, with as much other security as Elnon had, unless you were expecting trouble from people experienced at bypassing such systems, or willing to just blow them up in the process of the breaking part of breaking and entering.

One more note in the symphony. One more knot she had to undo, to make the galaxy safe again.

ART CRITIC

"SO GOOD TO SEE YOU AGAIN," Gareth heard as the auto-taxi dropped him in front of Elnon Ruaidhrí's mansion and flew off again.

Gareth waved and climbed those steps to greet the man at the door. As *Accord* bipeds went, Elnon was giant, but he was a Vanir, and they all were, for the most part. He probably outweighed Gareth by four stone, in spite of being several inches shorter, but Elnon looked like a pudgy, middle-aged businessman, not a field agent who needed to keep in top shape at all times.

They shook hands and Elnon escorted him to the back patio, where the early afternoon sun was just peeking over the building to keep things light but not yet hot. It had dawned an exceptionally gorgeous day, and promised to remain so clear up until sunset, when forecasters promised a fine mist to water everything.

Lunch was something Gareth called steak in his mind, served with something approximating fried mushrooms, at least by texture, and covered over with a rich demi-glace that was better than anything Gareth had ever had. The vegetables on the side were blue or yellow, crunchy, and pan-seared in butter.

It wasn't from a cow, but Gareth was past the point of comparing. They served the same purpose and even produced a similar-enough milk to make cheese and butter. Especially when you had a fantastically gifted chef on staff, apparently with instructions to impress a reporter wanting to let you show off your art collection to the universe.

Gareth belched appreciably and sipped a mug of coffee cut with chocolate and heavy cream in the Italian style.

"Wow," he said, letting that sum up lunch.

Elnon's smile turned up at both ends.

"So how else might I bribe you, old chap?" the art collector asked.

"I spoke with my editor," Gareth replied, referring to Eveth Baker even in his mind that way. "She would like me to get three or four good shots of places like the library and your bedroom, done in such a way that none of your security systems are obvious, so we don't advertise to the common criminal how to crack the place and make off with everything."

"The common criminal, Gareth?" he asked with a wicked tone to his voice.

"I presume that expert art thieves already know about your collection and have possibly tried their luck more than once, but either failed or were simply scared off."

"A little of both," Elnon laughed. "Not all the systems are obvious, and a few times, we have captured such criminals, but generally we don't advertise. But why the bedroom? There's nothing particularly noteworthy there. I prefer simple walls to art."

"There is nothing simple nor common about your bathroom, Ruaidhrí," Gareth laughed in turn. "Remember, in addition to art, we are selling a lifestyle. Your master bathroom is slightly larger than the biggest apartment I've ever had. Granted, I'm constantly traveling on assignment and single, so my needs tend towards the compact, but our readers like to be titillated with what the fabulously wealthy do with their money, while your competitors will suddenly demand that their interior decorator rip everything out and upgrade it, just to be better than yours."

That bolt struck home, as Gareth had known it would.

The rich all seemed to be alike in that way. Either they prefer to live simple, quiet lives where they alone knew they had money, or they actively competed with one another for ostentation. Take Gonquah and his yacht that was larger than Gareth's first independent command, the space-based Patrol Cutter *Bellerophon*, back on Earth. And the yacht never left the surface of that one planet.

"Oh, and perhaps a few shots of your vehicle collection would be useful as well," Gareth tossed that note in there nonchalantly. "Show everyone you are a well-rounded man of culture, and not just an art collector with some interesting paintings."

For a moment, Elnon's eyes grew dark and menacing, but then the gist of the phrase got through and he suddenly smiled.

"Yes, indeed," Elnon agreed. "This is so much more than merely art. It is, as you said, an entire lifestyle. Come, let us be off."

Gareth let go of the breath he had been holding and followed the man back into the building. As before, he counted steps carefully, building a three dimensional map in his head of the layout, but didn't bother pulling out his camera until they were upstairs and in that fantastic library.

Gareth fussed, asking questions and looking through the viewfinder as the sun lit the room with just the perfect amount of sunlight to add a line of whiteness to the air. He had wanted that early Eldritch Period piece, just because he couldn't find it any catalog, so it was either bought directly from the artist that many centuries ago, or had ended up here without any provenance at all.

"There," Gareth said, turning the camera around after he had gotten three or four good snaps for the folks back home to use in the future magazine article. "Do you think that captures the essence of the room? I'm thinking that might be the perfect image to lead with, setting you up as a most serious expert, reaching back centuries with the collection."

Elnon smiled proudly as he looked at the image on the screen.

"Yes," he said. "Elegant and subtle. What else would make the article pop?"

"I'd like to get one of you in your office, perhaps reviewing some meaningless paper of some sort at that desk," Gareth continued. "You, conveying forcefully that this is serious business that you must handle personally, instead of, as some others, merely hiring minions and giving them a budget to stock your domicile. Let's separate the serious collector from the poseur."

Again, the man preened, but Gareth understood how to play to Elnon's ego. Part of the journalist's job in something like this was to specifically make the subject look good. To make others jealous and competitive. To give the average wage-earner in their cubicle something to aspire to, or at least dream about.

Because the several magazines that carried Gareth's fictitious byline were all about the aspirational. The *Dream*. Even the Constabulary's help, secretly and quietly providing a significant amount of the funding for it, the folks running the magazine would go broke if they only sold to other elites, interested in outdoing one another. No, the money was in that dream.

In a way, Gareth had to crush the guilt he felt at peddling such a dream to folks that would never achieve it. At the same time, however, this was a much less destructive form of escapism, if he had to pick one, compared to say narcotics or alcohol. In that, he supposed that he was doing a public benefit. And that would make it all right.

The office had not changed. Four solid walls, lined with wood paneling rubbed a dark, rich mahogany that gleamed in the light of the desk lamp. There were no plants in here, but several bookshelves contained both knick-knacks and obviously-treasured tomes of some personal value.

"You sit there," Gareth directed. "Let me find the shot that makes you look the most heroic, and then I'll have you put on your serious face."

Elnon gladly sat, using a thumbprint to open a

drawer in the massive desk and pull out a small stack of papers. Gareth didn't bother even glancing at them. Instead, he knelt down and looked at the walls behind his target. Framing the shot.

Looking at the space, there was an area just behind Elnon on his left where there were no bookcases, and only a small trash can designed to hold whatever Elnon needed disposed of, rather than having a flame-chute to immediately annihilate something with fire. Considering his bulk, the other gaps in corners and cases would be too tight a fit, if you wanted to open a concealed door and vanish from sight in a hurry.

Gareth lined up the shot in his mind, and the aimed the camera.

"Now, can you look down and frown seriously, sir?" he asked, snapping several quick images as the man complied.

To take advantage of the light, Gareth shifted to his side and snapped more. And then stood.

"I'm not sure the standing shots will work, but they might also capture your struggle against the entire galaxy, so I'd like a few, just in case," Gareth called.

Somewhere, probably from his mother, he had apparently gotten an eye for this sort of thing, because half a dozen images all looked like keepers to him. An art editor would make that decision, but at least they would have something to work with.

"Perfect," Gareth said, showing him the shots. "Even the overhead ones convey strength. I think my editor would be pleased. How about your bedroom and the bath, next?"

They moved on, and Gareth was pretty sure he

could confirm the dead space. Eveth Baker had decided it was too risky to bring in any sort of portable scanner, camouflaged as something else, so Gareth had to just rely on intuition and whatever images he could get.

Nothing would be obvious, that much was clear. The man would have hidden any switches in such a way that even random chance would not reveal them. But at the same time, Gareth wouldn't need to break in this way, if they could access the space from below.

He could only hope.

And that damned bathroom had lost nothing on the second pass. He expected a number of folks would unhappily call their interior decorator after seeing these pictures and then make impossible demands about out-doing it. In that, his article on Elnon Ruaidhrí would be successful, if they ever ran it.

Wouldn't be of much value of course, if the man was in prison. Unless his wife was clean, and somehow managed to keep it in the face of Constabulary Auditors with green eyeshades and sharp pencils.

And Gareth managed a couple of good shots of the bedroom that just happened to catch the open closet door. Nothing much in there, except a confirmation of depth, side by side.

Downstairs, they went.

Gareth took a moment to use the main floor restroom as they did, partly because he'd had a lot of good coffee, and partly to measure that column of space against his memory. It only stood out because it made the room an awkward shape. All things considered, the man might have been better off moving a couple of other walls sideways, just so he could have a regular bathroom that didn't stand out in someone's memory like this.

As far as vehicles went when they got the underground garage, it was obvious that Elnon wasn't particularly interested in them. At least, not to the depth of some of the gearheads Gareth had known back home, or here in the *Accord*.

Xiomber, for example, would nerd out about private vehicles at the drop of a hat. They were rare in most cities, since auto-taxis could get you anywhere on short notice, including to orbit and across a wormhole tube, if you asked. But at the same time, not everyone wanted one, and they were not a requirement. Few people had or even needed their own car or flying sled to get around.

In that, Elnon showed money, but not much interest. He had a sleek, two-seater job in midnight blue that just screamed speed, especially from the way the landing gear would fold up into the bottom and give you smooth lines.

A larger vehicle was obviously intended to transport the man and his wife or business associates in luxury, facing each other across a small table where they could talk in comfort or negotiate in privacy. Beyond that, the *Accord* equivalent of a four-door sedan, presumably for the rarely-seen Mrs. Ruaidhrí to go places and do things.

Finally, a big box on wheels. Must be for hauling heavy loads around, except that the staff didn't look like the type. Perhaps, like an auto-taxi, you could dispatch it to pick something up, instead of relying on a delivery service to get around to you.

Still, for two people, an impressive garage. Gareth assumed that the nearly-invisible staff largely stayed in the other wing of the building from the master, and came and went via auto-taxi like normal people.

But it let him get significant pictures down in the underground space, including the ramp up and out the side, several sets of staircases, some of which were outdoors instead of into the building itself.

Pacing things off, Gareth also located a space that was surrounded by a small box of cyclone fencing, rather like where some office buildings would have people store bicycles out of the way in a parking garage. And it was in the right place for the rest of the column he was seeking, so Gareth walked all the way around to get the most shots.

"Why the vehicles, anyway?" Elnon asked as Gareth wrapped things up. "There's nothing particularly impressive here, as cars were never my thing."

"True, but consider how many people out there have never owned any private vehicles themselves, relying instead on auto-taxis and public transport their whole lives," Gareth nodded. "You have a stable, so you have wealth. At the same time, it's not that hollow ostentation that will turn some people off. As you said, you're not all about fast cars, too, so that will make you more personable, more impressive when they see the rest."

Gareth fixed him with a cold, calculating eye that was more journalist and art critic than cop. It felt weird, but it was also important.

"They want to pretend to be you, Ruaidhrí," he said firmly. "So you must be intimidating and fierce, but you must also be approachable, if they ever suddenly become fabulously wealthy themselves and run into you casually. That's the dream we sell. That's why people will buy the magazine. Does that make sense?"

Elnon paused for a moment, introspective.

"It does," he replied. "I just don't think I've ever run into someone with your level of passion for both the art and the journalism. If I get interviewed, they rarely know much, as this is just an assignment between doing a library opening and a wedding."

"More the fool them," Gareth let his own face turn to a scowl that wasn't pretend. "However, you have been most gracious, letting me take up your time this afternoon. I think I have what I need at this point, and my current schedule assumes that I'll have something written up for a quick review by your folks in about three weeks, if that works?"

"That would be lovely," he replied. "I'll be at a conference in a few days, and gone for about a week all told, so that timing lets me handle my other business first."

Gareth continued small talk as the man graciously ushered him out the front door, to a waiting auto-taxi.

As he rose into the sky, Gareth finally let himself smile. If the man was truly going to be gone, and Baker and Grodray would have the resources to confirm that, that would make his task so much easier.

And he might still write everything up. If the Constabulary seized everything, they would need to know how to value such a rare and probably priceless collection.

At least they had an expert on hand.

PORTALS

IT WAS A HACK JOB. Marc was aware of that, but it didn't really matter, as long as it worked.

Zorge and Maiair had brought in a couple of mechanics who worked under the table for the usual bribes, and they had assembled everything quickly enough, once the last bits of material were picked up from the middlemen.

And the suppliers had been willing to fall for the story about Marc needing to have a full set of spare parts up front. That, or perhaps they had understood that it would be easier to do this the first time given the political climate, rather than trying to order replacements later at a time when that was getting more and more difficult.

He had a full wormhole generator system now. Two of them, in fact. One packed up, back in crates after they had confirmed that everything worked, and the second pair assembled to make a full unit. Power would always be a problem, but an emergency system like this had two backup generators to power it, both topped off with enough fuel to last him a long time if he was careful enough to steal more later.

Marc laughed to himself that one of the tiny machines could probably output more power than the oversized, fusion reactors on either of Sky Patrol's primary LaGrange bases, despite being small enough to fit in a steamer trunk. But that would be necessary. Once he stepped through a portal and emerged on Earth, this system would destroy itself and nobody would be able to open it again. Or track where he'd gone.

If something went wrong, he'd be stuck on Earth for the rest of his life. Or at least until Constable Grodray found him. Or Gareth. His comrades would become freak-show performers, assuming the xenophobic peasants back home didn't just kill them out of fear or spite.

Sure, he could easily conquer Earth Force with his new technology, but who wanted to be king of an anthill just outside the walls of Versailles?

"What's so funny?" Maiair asked as the machine wound down from the latest calibrations tests.

The room wasn't all that crowded right now. He and the two Warreth females. The two Nari men. A Grace mechanic and his Vratha journeyman. Everyone else was at the far end of the garage space with the equipment, leaving him space.

"Playing out scenarios in my mind," Marc replied, letting some of the humor remain on his face for her to read. "I imagined all of us trapped on Earth when something went wrong, and having to settle for conquering that whole system for now."

"The Constables would still chase us, correct?" she asked. "Even there?"

"Even there," Marc assured her. "I'm sure they have agents in place somehow. Or at least watchers listening in on the radio signals, so they could report back quickly enough if something like us suddenly conquered Earth."

"You could always turn back into a human, Maximus," Maiair suggested. "That might let you hide. You'd be one grain of sand on a beach."

"I won't settle, Maiair," he growled back. "Everything, or nothing. And we won't be gone long. Just enough to set up a secret base in the Earth system, and I know many places we could do that. Then some recruiting and training, once we break my old comrades to the bit that there really are aliens out there."

"And then Empire?"

"Correct, First Wife," he smiled down at her. "Empire."

The sound was dropping to nothing in the rest of the space as the machines were finally wound down. The Grace mechanic approached, somehow conveying serious respect for Marc while maintaining the sort of attitude that showed he wasn't that impressed.

Marc nodded. A fine balance to strike.

"That's it for now," the man said simply. "We were able to target *Datha* with the scanners and pull something through. That's a representative shot over galactic distances, so everything should be ready. I'd run some more tests, if I were you, at least until so you're comfortable, before you put people through, but you don't need us for that."

He nodded back to his assistant.

"Zorge," Marc called. "You have everything you need?"

"We do," the Nari scientist replied.

Marc pulled an envelope from his inner pocket and handed it to the Grace with a smile.

"Thank you," he said. "We'll be in touch if something arises, but otherwise, I wish you the best of luck with your future."

And he meant it. Good technicians like this were rare. If Marc had just paid him the rough equivalent of two year's salary for this job, that just meant that the Grace would be able to enjoy better vacations or a better home. A better life, for not always having to play by the rules.

Quickly enough, Zorge got the two gone, leaving the inner gang alone.

"Understand this," Marc said. "Our next stop, once Zorge is ready, is a remote hiding place on *Earth*, in the Rocky Mountains not all that far removed from where I was born. Many of the back country places are accessible year around, but we should be timing this to arrive in the hardest part of winter, so the snows will be heavy and people will not be moving around."

"How do we know nobody will be there when we arrive?" Yooyar asked, coming up on her sister's other side.

"We don't," Marc assured her. "But the place I'm planning for has been used by underground gangs for a long time, so anyone we meet there will either be someone we can talk to, or someone we'll need to kill anyway. There will be no cops. And hopefully no sleeping bears."

"Sleeping bears?" Maiair asked, her crest ruffled. "How dangerous can they be?"

"They'll be a foot or two taller than me, covered over with thick fur, and weigh twice as much," Marc grimaced. "Grizzly bears hibernate by sleeping most of the winter, but they rouse occasionally, and can be angry and violent when they do. Shoot them without hesitation, if we encounter one. Understood?"

"This unit understands," the android said.

Everyone else had nodded, so it was a little jarring. Normally, the Ellis device was silent, but had apparently accepted those orders. Which was good. He could trust the killer robot to take down a grizzly.

"Okay, then," Marc concluded. "More tests on the wormhole machine, and then we'll need to figure out how soon we can depart. The next phase of our destiny awaits."

WALK IN THE PARK

ROYSTON HAD HOPED that by coming in to King's Cross station via Manchester and avoiding Westminster, they might be safe. After all, Camden Town had never lost its Bohemian nature, even as the rest of London itself had gentrified, renovated, faded, and reinvented itself over the centuries.

They had taken two rooms above a lovely, old Jazz café that still played live music every night, not all that far from St. Martin's Gardens. After breakfast, the three of them had taken a quick walk around Regent's Park on the Outer Circle, admiring the Zoo but not entering.

Royston had no idea how Terran animals might react to the smells of an alien Grace, and had no interest in finding out. Instead, they had continued the circle, arriving close to London's semi-ancient Central Mosque, where he and Fatima could murmur quietly back and forth. It wasn't her religion, or her heritage, but the woman she was impersonating was duly impressed and knowledgeable, which made it a pleasant experience.

At least until he turned and saw the figure almost stomping towards them on the sidewalk.

"And why, pray tell me, was I not informed you were in town, Loughty?" Sir West demanded as he got within yelling range.

Well, shit.

"Sir West, you remember my daughter, Philippa?" Royston asked as the man came to an angry halt in front of them. Royston pretended to ignore the rage seething off the man. "And may I present Ms. Fatima Darzi, niece of our old friend Firuz Alinejad?"

That deflected him, at least a little bit. Anger might be one thing, but good manners went bone deep with Sir West. Especially as both women were in Women's Auxiliary uniforms.

"Charmed," the old man said with a formal nod, vaguely mollified for the moment.

"Fatima, this is Dr. Sir Westfield van Duren-Abbott," Royston introduced her. "Professor Emeritus of Mathematics at King's College. Fellow of the Royal Society. Past Guardian of the Mathematical Union. Knight Grand Cross, Order of the British Empire. Knight Commander, Order of the Bath. My mentor and a dear friend of Firuz in the old days."

"A pleasure, Sir Westfield," Fatima replied, unsure what to say, obviously, since she could not know if the other Fatima had ever met Sir West in a previous life.

That had already tripped her up once with him. Royston stepped in to protect her.

Now was most assuredly not the time to expand their little conspiracy.

"And?" Sir West focused his ire on Royston again.

The man looked every one of his eighty-three years, with a wild ring of white hair surrounding a sea of liver spots on the bald top. Royston thought that Sir West's tweeds today might be older than Royston was. At least Pippa. The eyes were normally hazel, perhaps raging over into bronze today, and gave lie to the rest of the man's unkempt appearance as a fussy old duffer headed down to the pub for a pint.

"And we just arrived last night, Sir West," Royston tried to placate the man.

At least a little.

Royston wasn't going to let the man push too far. He was on vacation, after all. Even if it might take the form of saving the galaxy from hostile, alien invasion. Royston was still going to enjoy himself, damn it.

"What brings you north this morning, Sir West?" Pippa stepped forward and demurely injected her femininity into the conversation like a delicate perfume.

"Eh? Oh, consulting at Regent's University this month," Sir West took his anger down a notch. "Teaching a small group of advanced students in a special class on calculating the mathematical shape of space as gravity wells intersect."

"Fascinating," Pippa smiled at him. "We're secretly on vacation, but don't tell Alvin that. He thinks we've gone off to find more of Father's magical mathematical equations."

Royston nearly laughed out loud, but managed to contain it. Pippa could probably teach the class along with Sir West. She was certainly doing advanced, post-doctoral work, even if no serious college would ever admit her or Fatima into their graduate programs.

More the fools them.

Sir West focused his eyes on Royston, with silent Fatima nearly forgotten in the background, as intended.

"Alvin tells me that there's a flaw in your math?" the old man of science demanded.

"Perhaps, old friend," Royston allowed. "Remember, when I built the device we both concluded that significant portions of the equations had too large an error factor. Experimental evidence was necessary to see where we hadn't gone far enough."

"Blow up the Earth, Loughty?" Sir West's voice rose, just a bit louder.

"Oh, I don't think the probability gets much above about two percent right now, Sir West," Royston grinned. "Still, that's far too high, all things considered."

"And sneaking off to London?" he demanded. "Alvin said you were in Nevada, of all places."

"It made a useful cover story, Sir West," Royston replied. "What I'm really about right now is finding that young woman musician, and seeing if I can coax lightning to strike a second time."

"There is no space in proper mathematics for black magic, Loughty," Sir West growled, rather like a chipmunk threatening a terrier.

"Agreed, Sir West," Royston let his smile widen. "And yet, look where it has gotten us so far. We might be on the brink of another complete social and cultural revolution in human history, if it proves truly possible to lift a payload into orbit without a rocket. After that, it becomes a question of reach, but the math on the power necessary suggests something like an inverse square or perhaps an inverse cube of distance, so we'll be a considerable amount of time before we might be able to deposit a man on the Saturnine Gas Mining colony."

"You will keep me more regularly updated, young man," Sir West threatened. "And the day after tomorrow I was scheduled to have tea at Buckingham. You will attend, and provide Her August Majesty with your latest findings. Am I understood?"

"You are, Sir West," Royston bowed, chagrined. "We will contact your office down in The City and get the details tomorrow. Today, however, I damned well intend to enjoy myself as a tourist. That means the Wellington Arch and Nelson's Column shortly, followed by the National Galleries. So be off with you to go torture your poor students."

Sir West bowed to the two women and departed, somewhat chagrined at Royston's own snappiness.

"Well, that went about as bad as I had feared," Pippa said as the man moved off, finishing an apparent morning constitutional, clock-wide around Regents.

"Indeed, daughter," Royston said. "The worst possible luck, but we will just have to make the best of it at the time when it can no longer be avoided."

"Is a visit to the Queen really that terrible, Royston?" Fatima finally broke her silence.

"No," Royston sighed, offering his elbows to the two women so they could walk some more. "It means that we'll be more under surveillance, however well-meaning it might be. We won't be able to just come and go as we please, at a time when I'd like to enjoy my old home town as something more of an innocent. At least one last time."

"I'm not sure I understand, Royston," Fatima's brow furrowed.

"If we fail, all of this will be gone, Fatima," he said. "Returned to a decaying wilderness as man disappears and the animals slowly reclaim it over the next few millennia. No more Mozart or Tchaikovsky, but also no more rock and roll."

That would probably be the worst part, stripping away the future from all these innocents around them, to die unknowing of his failure, but to die nonetheless.

Both women seemed to understand and leaned a little into him as they walked.

UNINVITED GUEST

GARETH WASN'T sure how to ascribe it, but he was willing to offer thanks for the blessing of Tyche, Roman Goddess of Luck. Both of the Ruaidhrí's had departed to attend the conference on *Churquark*, leaving the mansion largely empty.

According to surveillance teams and data collectors, about half the staff had gotten a long weekend, so there was almost nobody in the mansion. And, happily, no dogs. Gareth had a stunner, just in case, as well as a heavy disintegrator pistol, on the off-chance he encountered another Ellis device.

Not all of the killer androids had been accounted for, according to Gonquah's detailed construction records. And they still haunted his nightmares, from time to time.

The exterior of mansion was dark and the moons were both down. Plus there was the promise of rain later, so the sky was dark. Gareth had broken in to

Gonquah's factory at Baker's side, and she had decided to repeat that process.

Instead of relying on lifterpacks, however, she was relying on Gareth.

They stood on a nearby block, in a darkened park that was closed at sunset. Both wore their blue-gray bodysuits with built-in scale armor, and dual holsters loaded for bear. Or at least dogs and androids. Grodray had a smaller team than last time, but just as heavily armed, plus more people on call in an emergency.

"Ready?" Gareth asked, glancing around, but he could see no witnesses.

Eveth smiled up and him and nodded.

Gareth took a step back and triggered the transformation into the Star Dragon. It was growing less painful each time, which was good. It was also bad, because he found himself looking forward to the other form. One of these days, he might not to come back to the alien form of a Vanir. What would he do then?

And yes, his eyes seemed a little higher this time, compared to his memory of Baker before. He really was still growing. What would he turn into at this rate?

Eveth turned her back to Gareth as they had practiced and relaxed as his paws came up and encircled her torso. He tried not to think about how he was holding her. And he was happy that a Star Dragon couldn't blush. At least visibly.

"Taking off," Gareth said. "Deep breath."

He could feel her draw the air in through is fingers and he tightened his hold, taking his own breath as he lifted her up and got a running start forward.

It was awkward, with her seventeen stone weight forward of his usual center of gravity, but he adjusted. Plus, it wasn't like he needed to set any speed records here. Just fly her two blocks over and land quietly near a side door, in a part of the mansion where they should be invisible. Still, bringing in lifterpacks would have been awkward, while walking, and would have signaled a problem if they left them outside the building.

Good thing he could fly.

Eveth Baker kept her muscles rigid as he flew, arms down and toes pointed so she didn't flail any.

Just like that, he was silently circling as he judged his landing. Even the quietest auto-taxi made more noise, but his wings flapped as though a large bird.

"Ready?" he repeated himself, quietly.

"Go," Baker replied.

Gareth relaxed and let the instincts Talyarkinash and the Yuudixtl brothers had programed take over. His tail came down as he fought to hover. He couldn't but it let him land like a javelin, rather than requiring a long, swooping pass. Baker's toes touched the turf almost as fast as he did, and then Gareth began to transform back.

At least the shift didn't involve him glowing. That would be weird. Okay, weirder.

How weird was it to turn into a dragon in the first place?

Gareth drew both pistols and backed up against the side of the building. They were below the level of the first floor windows, and thick hedges and trees blocked off any view of from the neighbors.

Baker seemed to be picking the lock with her eyes closed. Seriously. He checked.

She had explained the process to him once, the touch, but he hadn't practiced it. He saw his future either kicking in the door with an arrest warrant, or as a public, secret agent worming his way into the corrupt niches of wealth and breeding that had accumulated over the centuries.

Art Critic was as good as anything else he could have come up with.

The door clicked open, but all she did was turn the knob to confirm she had succeeded. Now she pulled out a small scanner and ran it over the entire frame. That was complicated, since the door was down in a small well, three steps below ground level, but she didn't seem to mind getting dirty.

The device in her hands beeped once and she grunted. Quickly, she pulled a small boring laser from one of her belt pouches and small camera. Gareth listened to all the night sounds, but wanted to watch her work, glancing up occasionally.

Eveth set the beam on a particular spot and quickly drilled a hole in the door frame, into which went the camera.

"Good," she muttered as she studied the tiny screen. "There."

Gareth heard a clicking sound so quiet he might have imagined it, but she pulled the camera back out of the hole and slid everything into pockets. She drew her stunner and glanced at him.

"Grodray. Step one," she said, letting the microphone built into her suit transmit the words.

Grodray wouldn't reply, but his team would know where they were.

Gareth grinned. She had drilled in, located a simple electrical circuit, and jumped it, so opening the door wouldn't break the existing circuit and sound an alarm. Nifty, but Gareth presumed that a cat burglar would do something similar. So the next step was probably where they tripped.

She pulled the door open and listened for bells or something to indicate an alarm. Grodray's team had someone on a Constabulary circuit, ready to interrupt the local police if they got an alarm and came to investigate.

Into the garage, pulling the door closed behind them. There was enough light down here to see, even at night. Gareth had noted the light levels earlier, so they didn't need complicated helmets to work right now.

Over to that cage.

Baker surprised him by simply sticking a key into the lock on the cyclone-fencing door and turning. It popped right open.

"Polymorphic master key," she grinned at his confusion. "I was able to identify the lock maker from your images, so I programmed something ahead of time."

Huh. This woman was even sneakier than he had thought.

Gareth turned himself sideways and watched the basement door where someone up in the kitchen would emerge. No word from Grodray meant no exterior alarms to this point, but someone might have gotten a silent ping upstairs and come down to see what was happening, even if the exterior didn't sound.

Maybe a rabbit had wandered in earlier and

settled down, and was now frantically trying to escape the garage?

This was when things got interesting. He watched Eveth pull a larger scanner from her belt and begin to quarter the walls inside the storage unit.

"Bingo," she said quickly. "Helps knowing that he's Vanir."

She was pointing to a simple section of pipe that emerged from the wall at head level, and came down to a faucet with a twist-grip to open and close it. Water to wash off your hands, since there was a drain right below it.

Baker turned the knob and nothing came out. But behind her, the wall seemed to shift backwards. She put away the scanner and pushed on the wall.

"Grodray, that's two," she said, marking the next penetration step.

Still nothing on the airwaves, and nobody coming.

Baker nodded as an overhead light came on. Automatic, when this door was opened.

She went in first, and Gareth followed.

The space beyond was a narrow hallway, at least for a Vanir, that ended in a circular staircase going up.

"Close the door behind you," Baker ordered as she approached it, her scanner out again and pinging the space.

Gareth noted that this side of the heavy door had a simple handle, like any interior door, but it clicked firmly into place when he pushed. It was still built like a bank vault, to push it closed and feel the bolts set. And being inside a bicycle cage, nobody was likely to bump into it from the outside.

You had to know something was here. Or had strong suspicions and great need.

Hopefully, they were inside Elnon's security now. Since they weren't trying to steal any art from the walls, those sensors would be in rooms they did not need to visit.

"Grodray, confirm three," Baker said quietly.

They waited a moment, unsure now if their radios could penetrate the walls of the panic room.

"Confirm three," the Senior Constable said a moment later.

Gareth let go a soft sigh. Being out of contact wouldn't have scrubbed the mission, but it meant that he and Baker might get killed without anyone being able to rescue them, as had almost happened last time.

Paranoia in this business was not always bad.

From the look on Baker's face, she felt the same way.

"Climbing stairs," Baker said aloud, putting her scanner away, apparently satisfied, and aiming her stunner up and forward.

Gareth followed, making even less noise than the professional cat burglar in front of him.

Interestingly, there was a door on the ground floor, visible from this side. The whole front of the column would apparently hinge open, letting you escape from upstairs. Or perhaps just offering Elnon a quiet way to get to the ground floor. Old castles and manor houses on Earth had something similar, but that was generally for kings and folks to sneak between bedrooms at night.

Gareth wondered if Elnon had the need. Or just had hired an architect who believed in completeness.

If you were in the Grand Salon, this was close enough to flee to, and you could lock the outer door, at least long enough to disappear from someone who didn't think about secret doors.

Up again they circled. The next floor was the panic room he had expected, but the stairwell continued up. Apparently, the master could exit into the attic, or perhaps he kept a pair of lifterpacks stored up there for a daring getaway.

A small bed in one corner. Only big enough for one person, which perhaps said something about Elnon that hadn't been obvious before. A small kitchenette, like you frequently found in nicer hotels, complete with a refrigerator block. A desk where Elnon could work.

A whole wall of fireproof filing cabinets, five drawers tall, since they were a standard size and Vanir scaled. Six of them, each three feet deep. Locked, but it was another simple lock. Mechanical as the others had been.

That made sense. If someone managed to kill the power to the building, you didn't want everything electronic to die with it. The alarms probably had some sort of uninterruptable power supply, good for days if you were serious. But the master would want to escape, and use his own muscles, especially if everything was off.

Baker tapped one of the cabinets, but returned to the stairwell, taking the first stride and nodding back at him.

Gareth followed her up. He had been right. The attic had been rearranged into a small flight bay. However, instead of lifterpacks, there was another small speeder up here. Not as impressive externally as the one downstairs, but Gareth suspected that this one was probably one of the fastest you could buy.

A man like Elnon, if pressed that close, would want to run hard and fast, and wouldn't skimp here. Not with as much money as he had spent downstairs to acquire his art.

"And none of this exists in any of the architectural drawing submitted to the city fire department," Baker murmured.

"Come again?" Grodray was on the line.

"Transmitting an image," she laughed, stepping back and pulling out a camera. "Slightly modified attic."

When Grodray whistled, they dropped back down a level. Gareth holstered his stun pistol and just settled for being able to kill androids and small vehicles. Baker could outdraw him if she needed to, and someone coming along now needed to be taken down quietly.

Or blown into smoldering, metallic wreckage.

THIEF IN THE NIGHT

EVETH STUDIED the panic room that Elnon Ruaidhrí had assembled. It was impressive, especially with all the other things she had known about the man. Stuff not even Gareth had been told, thus far. His whole life was probably locked up in these cabinets. Every piece of art. Every crime. Every bribe. And nobody had ever suspected anything until Gareth came along a year ago.

Some days, she wondered if he was blessed by the *Chaa*. Certainly, his advent into her life had altered everything. Maybe they had sent him as a quiet way to save everything, so they didn't have to come in and crack heads together.

Eveth had never been particularly religious, especially compared to many others, but some days, she questioned that.

They had been trying to nail Ruaidhrí for decades, and failing. In just a few weeks, Gareth had the man dead to rights.

"Where would you put the important papers,

Gareth?" she turned to her new lucky charm and asked.

Gareth surprised her by holstering his disintegrator, his own lucky charm piece after Gonquah, and sitting at Elnon's desk. Both big hands went flat on the top for a moment, and then he rotated to his left, standing and taking one long stride to the cabinets at the farthest end of the room.

"This one," Gareth tapped that stack.

"Why?" she asked, intrigued.

"When he sat at his desk, this was the way he had to turn to open that door," Gareth pointed. "So I'm guessing it is a natural motion."

She nodded at the sound logic and slipped her picks into the keyhole at the top. She had read Gareth's report about a fingerprint pad in the office, but everything in here relied on mechanical rather than electronic solutions. Probably a key in the desk in here, which was also locked with a thumbprint, when she glanced back.

This lock took some effort. She was almost sweating when she finally got all the tumblers to surrender, although just cutting the damned thing out with her laser was still an option. An admission of surrender on her part, but an option.

She pulled the massive top drawer out and looked at the file folders contained. The front one caught her eye, and apparently her partner's as well.

"Damn it," Gareth murmured under his breath, reaching in and drawing it out.

Eveth followed the big Vanir agent back over to the desk and looked over his shoulder as he laid it flat and opened it.

"Grodray, stand by for action," she said simply.

"What's up?" he asked back.

"We are reviewing a file with Sarzynski's name on it," she said. "And he…crap. Oh, that's very bad."

"Talk to me, Eve," Grodray's voice got sharp.

"I need you to call it in and send a high level messenger off to *Churquark* faster than the news can get there. And then get here and quietly arrest all the staff," Eveth said. "From this file, Elnon sold Maximus all the parts that man needs to build himself two wormhole stations."

"Repeat that, Baker?" Grodray said.

"I think maybe Morty was right. Sarzynski's going to Earth for an army, Jack," Eveth felt the dread take over her entire body.

HOME

THE PERSONAL WORMHOLE tube was nothing like riding in the comfort of an auto-taxi on the short blip to orbit. Those took almost no time at all to complete. This trip was measured in the number of heartbeats Marc had to count as he passed feet first down what his mind kept interpreting as a gullet. As though he were in the process of being swallowed by a whale.

Marc kept those thoughts to himself. This was not the time to be thinking about burning bushes, either, or messengers from God, however it might look when he landed on the other side.

Hopefully, there would be nobody there and he could get organized quietly before reaching out to some old contacts to see how much of the network had survived, after his disappearance almost two years ago.

Marc saw the end of the tunnel appear, racing madly towards him. He already held a stun pistol in hand, against need, and took a deep breath against the oppressive atmosphere around him.

And then he landed. Just as he had before. One moment, tunnel to infinity. The next, he had popped into existence. Rebirth, as conquest.

The Bunker had been built by a crime boss more than a century ago, taking over an abandoned mine in northern Colorado and turning the place into an oversized complex almost like one of the ancient missile silos that still dotted the plains north and east of here.

Rough walls had been polished just enough that you wouldn't cut yourself on them. Concrete floors had been poured and leveled by professionals at different heights, creating large slabs like a multi-deck patio or mod living room.

In one hand, Marc held his stunner. In the other, a flashlight, but it was unneeded, as the lights were on in the large space where he landed.

"Cripes, what the hell is that?" someone yelled.

Marc spun and aimed at the four men that had been playing poker at an old-fashioned wooden table.

"Cops," another of the men yelled.

Before Marc could say anything, the men all exploded into action, reaching for pistols in belts or shoulder holsters.

There was no time to discuss this like rational beings, so Marc just opened fire, dropping the men like flies onto the table or floor. He paused as the they were down, looking around.

The space was large and open, almost vaulted like a church, with a number of doors along one side, opposite an area where a kitchen had been built. One of those doors began to open now.

"What's going on?" a man asked.

Marc shot him, too, and then raced to the door. Inside, a woman began to scream. The stunner silenced her.

Down each door, Marc thrust them open from the side, looked in, and moved on when each proved empty.

A pulse of power drew his attention back to the main room. Maiair stepped through, followed by Yooyar a moment later. Both were armed and prepared. Marc had deliberately had them hold back thirty seconds, just in case something bad happened and he needed a surprise. Or if the people here had reacted in a civilized manner, and not like criminals.

Of course, civilized people didn't even know this place existed, but Marc was playing with the cards he was dealt.

"Any more of them?" Maiair asked, covering a large door near the kitchen.

"Not on this side," he replied. "That's the garage. You check there and I'll clear the storage areas."

There was a small thorium reactor buried on one side of the next room under a protective shield. The other side held a massive cistern of pressurized water brought up from deep below. In between were a number of boxes and crates that held the sorts of sundries a man might need if he was going to hide out from the cops for a month or two, plus a pair of massive, walk-in units, one a freezer filled with meat and vegetables, and the other merely a refrigerator, also packed.

The men and women out there weren't going hungry. Nor would Marc's team, with the supplies that would be transported over.

He returned to the main room as the two Warreth women were locking the garage door from this side.

"What do we do with them?" Yooyar asked, gesturing to the four stunned gangsters.

"Tie them up for now," Marc said, as well the two back in the first bedroom. "How long until Zorge comes through?"

"Two minutes, as you ordered," Maiair replied.

Marc nodded. It was good to be dealing with professionals.

They gathered up the six and used plastic ties to hook the men and woman to chairs. The girl had the look of a bimbo the boss had brought along: extremely pretty and barely eighteen from the look of her, when the boss was in his fifties and badly out of shape. Had she been dressed when Marc arrived, he might have given her the benefit of the doubt and perhaps suggested daughter, but she was also of Caribbean descent, a darker, richer brown compared to the pastier white of the rest.

At least the gunmen weren't slobs. And had reacted quickly and efficiently with violence. That they had no chance against Marc wasn't going to count too much against them.

Zorge appeared next, off to one side with a pistol in hand. He looked around at the situation and nodded.

"Gear next?" he asked Marc.

"That's right," Marc replied.

The Nari scientist turned and vanished.

About the time the gangsters were stirring, crates began to appear over in one corner, as though materialized by an invisible genie. The first android came over in one load, leaving Zorge with the other two and Mishalska for now.

"What gives?" one of the men asked as he woke up and looked around. "Some sort of Halloween thing?"

Marc walked over and smiled. He had to remember that he wasn't human any more. That they wouldn't see him as one of them, even if any had been people that might recognize him from before.

"I needed your base," he announced in perfect English, which felt weird after all the time he had spent in the *Accord*, speaking their tongue. "It was unfortunate that you were here, but maybe we can work something out with your boss, because I only plan to stay here a little while before I go home."

"Which of the Nine Hells is home, you monster?" the man asked. Clearly, he was the leader, as the others just watched silently.

"A planet you wouldn't know, halfway across the galaxy," Marc smiled.

Behind him, a particularly large box came through the golden portal with a loud sound as it pushed several tons of other equipment forward a few inches.

"Jesus, what is all that?" the man's eyes were almost all whites now. "What are you?"

"You wouldn't believe me," Marc said. "So remain quiet for now and listen when I talk to your boss. If you boys are good, nothing bad will happen to you. In fact, really good things might happen instead. *Capiche*?"

"Uhm, sure, buddy," the man said. "Whatever you say."

The girl awoke first, and started screaming. Marc

had to stun her to get her to shut up, and then tied a cloth around her mouth, making sure she could breathe, but not give him headaches.

The boss awoke last. Not surprising, since the effects of stun were best ameliorated by being healthy, and that fat little ball of anger was anything but.

He did remain more or less silent when he woke up, straining against this bonds even less effectively than the other four had.

"I'm going to boil the story down to the bits you need to know, understand?" Marc began, drawing all eyes in the room to him.

The two Warreth women didn't speak English, nor did the android, but they were mostly watching the prisoners for now. And ambushes that might occur.

"Two years ago, I was the boss known as Maximus," Marc's eyes bored in on the fat man. "Do you know that name?"

"Yeah," the little man replied. "But you ain't human."

"Correct," Marc said. "Something happened, and I got transformed into a race known as the Vanir. These two women are another race called Warreth."

All five sets of eyes turned to the women. Warreth might have feathers, bills, and head crests, but the Chaa had still made them mammalian bipeds on the same basic model as themselves. That Maiair and Yooyar were such exemplary examples just doubled the fascination of the men watching.

"The other is a combat-model android," Marc continued. "Fast enough to kill all of you before you even know what happened, so mind your manners. Am I understood clearly?"

All five nodded now. Cowed, perhaps.

"Good," Marc continued. "Two more men will join us shortly. They are Nari, and look like perhaps a Canadian Lynx, if you boys know what one of those are. As I said earlier, I needed your base. If you want to be cut in on my deal, I'm here to recruit a group of human killers, like I was, to help me go conquer the entire galaxy. The people out there are patsies. Pacifists, even, in some cases. But there are hundreds of planets of them, and I'm going to need gunmen like you to keep them in line."

"Aliens?" the fat boss asked quietly. "Like on the vid?"

Marc fought to keep the sigh and eyeroll contained. He was back in the bush leagues again, obviously. Surrounded by provincials and fools. One step at a time, trying to find enough straw to make bricks.

"Correct," Marc said. "I used to be human. They kidnapped me because they needed a killer. Now I'm in charge of the gang."

That got through to at least two of the mooks, the smart one at the far end of the poker table and one of the others. The sorts of men who understood what it meant to have an eye to the main chance. Those two moved up on his list to chat up individually.

"So why ain't you in charge over there?" the boss started like he was going to get smart.

"There are about a million cops in the *Accord*," Marc said. "Maybe ten million. It's a war, right now, and I'm one of the only killers. Even the two women here can't help me take on all that. Plus, those bastards went and got some help from Sky Patrol."

That got a good reaction from the four gunmen. All of them had probably seen the inside of a Sky Patrol jail at one time or another.

"Sky Patrol knows about all this?" the boss asked, incredulous.

"Parts of it do," Marc semi-lied to the men.

Gareth Dankworth was Sky Patrol, regardless of anything else. That was enough.

"So why are you here, Maximus?" the boss finally asked in a reasonable voice.

"I need an army of humans," Marc replied coldly. "Killers."

"An army?"

"Yes," Marc smiled. "You're going to help me conquer the galaxy."

IN HER MAJESTY'S SERVICE

ROYSTON APPROACHED this meeting like a duel in the old American West. High Noon Showdown, as it were. He had sent his best suit in for an emergency trip to the cleaners. Pippa and Fatima had broken out their best dress uniforms from storage.

Young Prince Henry of Wales greeted them at the door to the residential wing of the palace, once they had passed all the layers of security, armed or subtle, wrapped like layers of nacre around the place.

The young man had grown in the last year. He was probably nearly his father's height now, and would develop the man's breadth of shoulders soon. He looked down on Royston almost apologetically.

"Dr. Loughty," the young prince nodded to them. "Miss Loughty. Miss Darzi. Welcome."

He led them deeper into the palace, past more guards and functionaries than had been here before. They did not end up in the same, cozy chamber as before, but one closer to the Personal Quarters.

Royston wasn't sure if that made him feel better, or left him further on edge.

Through the door, he found Sir West seated to one side, and Prince Consort Daniel to the other. Her Majesty was seated at the center of a small arc, and the man next to her, opposite the Prince Consort, brought home to Royston just how dangerous the game had suddenly become.

Admiral Sir William Wellesley-Knox, *Commander, English Military Forces Earth* and a former Sky Marshall of Sky Patrol itself. That is, Operations Commander of the entire force.

Royston had tangled with the man a few times over the years, but the Admiral had been Sky Patrol, and Royston's appointments and chain of command had only been Earth Force for the last fifteen years or so, so the arguments had been civil and bureaucratic, rather than risking breaking out into fisticuffs on the corridor outside an especially heated meeting.

It had come close more than once, though.

The admiral was a tall, lean, and bluff man who still managed to look rather like a shopkeeper from Manchester with his stern gaze.

Pippa and Fatima were introduced and seated on Royston's flanks, like wingmen he might need in a dogfight. The symbolism was not lost on Royston.

Prince Consort Daniel served tea, as before. Sandwiches and biscuits as only the Queen might rate. Small talk on various irrelevancies. More tea was delivered in silence by efficient servants.

Her Majesty, Elizabeth III, studied Royston over the edge of her mug as she sipped, remaining mostly silent. The Crown Prince explained some of his studies into the sciences, in response to general questions from his father and Sir West.

Even Fatima was interrogated mildly, both by Sir West and Prince Henry, but it was obvious after a moment that Sir West had never met the real Fatima Darzi, so he was at very little risk of tripping up the imposter seated with him now. And the questions were more curiosity about Persia than anything particularly personal.

"Rock and roll music, Dr. Loughty?" Her Majesty asked suddenly. "That might be the key to our future?"

"It does seem rather daft, on the surface of things, I will grant," Royston was at pains to keep everything bright and cheerful, both tone and body language. "However, my usual inspirations of syncopated jazz or the classical masters had failed me for the very first time. With Pippa's assistance, I sought inspiration in other venues. Other avenues of art, if you will."

"And now?" the Queen pressed.

"And now I have given much thought to the physics and mathematics I have uncovered, madam," he said simply. "As I noted previously, some of the basic theory was simply wrong, based on subsequent experimental data. Or perhaps incomplete would more accurately describe it. I needed a break from my labors, so I thought to locate that woman who had so inspired me the first time, in an effort, as I explained to Sir West, to see if lightning might be induced to strike a second time."

"And she is in London now?" Her Majesty asked.

"She will be, shortly," Royston said. "Thus, my heretofore secret venture. But for Sir West stumbling upon us, we would have attended the show tomorrow night and then been off on other jaunts immediately afterwards, with none the wiser."

A glance passed between Sir William and the Queen now. Royston steeled himself for whatever foolishness was about to issue forth from the man's mouth and fixed his gaze on the admiral, as though daring him.

The Admiral did not shrink.

"Should she be invited to the palace for a private performance?" Sir William asked.

"Certainly," Fatima, of all people spoke up suddenly, her voice tart with brilliant, sarcastic innuendo. Amazing, especially since she wasn't even human, but she had the intonation perfect. "If your desire is to ruin the entire impact of what we are attempting. Sir William."

"I beg your pardon," the Admiral's ruff came up.

"It would be as useful as demanding you regale us with all the verses of *God Save The Queen, a capella,* right now," Fatima stuck the burning embers under the man's fingernails, at least metaphorically. "The purpose was to recreate the original night in question, with that woman in complete and utter control of the entire auditorium, both psychologically and emotionally. Anything else is just a waste of everyone's time. I was not there, yet I have felt the power of it, merely from the stories Royston and Pippa have told me. So no, you should not ruin this woman's harmony by demanding she dance for her supper."

Royston bit his tongue rather than laugh. This woman was only impersonating Fatima Darzi, but he could actually remember the original woman unleashing that tone of anger, doubly rare in a land where the only way a woman had any power at all was to be born into it. In that, Admiral Sir William Wellesley-Knox might represent everything that both Fatima Darzi and a young Grace woman named Ilak Vorta might find wrong with present, human society.

The room had fallen to a shocked silence.

All the more so because a Persian woman might say such a thing to an English officer. Some memories went back centuries, to a less enlightened time, when the United Kingdom had not behaved with any great honor. And Fatima had done her homework on the Nineteenth and Twentieth Centuries of Earth. And Anglo-Persian relations.

Royston had checked.

He sat quietly, waiting to be metaphorically thrown out of the palace for insulting Her Majesty's honor. Wars had begun over less.

Elizabeth Regina shocked him by grinning.

"Then perhaps Dr. Loughty might be induced to act *in loco parentis* instead," she said casually. "I expect that Prince Henry would find the performance enthralling, but, as you have noted, making a royal production of the event might despoil the very thing you sought."

As traps went, Royston found it masterful. The jaws were closed around his ankle before he even knew they were there. Prince Henry blushed. Prince Consort Daniel smiled. Sir William retained his gruff silence. They had all played their hands masterfully.

Royston couldn't remember the last time he had been ensnared so effectively. At least it had been Her Majesty that did it.

His honor could live with that.

"I would be delighted, Your Majesty," Royston surrendered gracefully. "The situation calls for subtlety, so the ladies with me were going to attend in mufti. If the Crown Prince's bodyguards were to maintain a discrete distance, none might even be aware that he had joined us. It will, of course, require utmost secrecy across the board. One hint to our supposed *Euterpe* of the gravity of the situation and all may be for naught, as she seemed to sense the power flowing in the air last time."

"So it shall be, Dr. Loughty," Her Majesty said with triumph in her voice.

Royston acquiesced, and hopes that nothing would go wrong, with an alien in their midst, magic poised to happen, and several dangerous men nearby with weapons.

He had simply run out of alternatives.

CONQUEST

GARETH HAD FOUND a new definition of professionalism that challenged every preconception he had ever had on the topic.

An entire Constabulary force had arrived at the front door, as well as every other entrance, and promptly and politely arrested everyone in the building, which came down to two maids, a groundskeeper, and the Ruaidhrí's personal chef. A maid, and butler, and a seneschal, for lack of a better description, had traveled with the Ruaidhrí's off-planet.

Security systems had been deactivated for now, but left intact, as the art in the building was still probably priceless and would need to be protected against theft. Plus, a small team of Gareth's new friends in the Art Fraud department had been called in and would remain on premises for the time being, cataloging and protecting the assembly.

There was one problem, however. The Chef simply refused to be arrested. Period.

She was a small Grace woman who somehow reminded Gareth of his maternal grandmother, both in their petite stockiness, and the fact that no stranger was allowed in the house without food in front of them.

So the entire team had moved down to the dining hall, minus only those people guarding the grounds or who had collected the rest of the staff and taken them away. Madam Streffa Vorkinnik was in the process of fixing what she called a quick snack for everyone.

If you were the kind of person who could just whip up a plate of chips covered with meat, cheese, and sauce, as a prelude to hot sandwiches, while cookies went into the stove. Two of the team had been detailed to oversee the Grace woman, lest she poison the team.

That had nearly gotten one of them slapped, when he made the mistake of saying it out loud.

Professionalism. Even in the face of being arrested under the possibility of being an accessory to treason.

And the cookies were delightful. Chocolate chip, more or less. Snickerdoodlish. And something closer to a sweet scone with dried fruit, that you dipped into a double cream.

And she had done it all from scratch, instructing her minders which jars to hand her and where to find the utensils. Without any recipe except experience.

Gareth burped as the first round of Italian-style sweet coffee arrived, flavored with chocolate and dulce de leche. He was just sorry he couldn't afford to hire this woman. Even for a day.

Grodray shared a commiserative smile as if he was thinking the same thoughts.

"What do we know?" Grodray asked.

All the eating was done at one end of the long table, with a towel stretched across the surface like a low curtain wall, to capture any spilled coffee that might threaten the stack of documentation at the other end.

Gareth had quickly sorted every folder into three, rough piles, pending their being scanned into evidence systems later when they forensics team arrived.

For now, he put his coffee down carefully and walked over to the smallest stack. The larger two were art documentation and histories of ownership, and Ruaidhrí's personal records, mostly running the manor house, but also certain things about the many companies he either owned or sat on the boards of.

"Old money," Gareth said simply. "Well organized financial systems in place, dating back at least four hundred years to conserve his wealth generationally. We know they have two, grown children, one just finished with university and the other a few years behind. Trust funds have been established, so neither are at risk of ending up on the streets, if they are found to be innocent of their father's misdeeds."

"And what can we prove in the short term?" Eveth Baker asked, always one to go straight for the throat.

"Selling illegal and unlicensed wormhole technology to known criminals," Gareth said. "Namely, Marc Sarzynski. And recently enough, in the last month or so. That is enough to take him away and begin stripping away the rest of the layers. As with Gonquah, I expect we'll be years finding everything, but one man can only serve one lifetime in prison, regardless of the number of life sentences a judge might hand down."

"And Maximus has everything he needed?" Grodray asked sharply.

Gareth shrugged, looking at the documentation.

"He had everything he ordered from Ruaidhrí," Gareth offered. "I am the last person to ask about tube station engineering."

Grodray nodded at him.

"Correct," he said. "But I know just who can fill in the blanks here."

The Senior Constable rose from the table and walked to the far end of the room, talking quietly into his pocketcomm.

"Do we know where?" Eveth asked in hushed tones.

"In my wildest dreams, I cannot imagine that the equipment was set up where it was delivered," Gareth said. "Nobody is that dumb, when working that far outside of the law. Stupid people would have already been caught."

"So this is a dead end?" she pressed.

"The hardware is, most likely, yes," Gareth agreed. "We have more names to dig out and arrest. All the deliveries took place on this planet, so somebody has seen Sarzynski. We just haven't asked them hard enough yet."

Gareth returned to his excellent coffee before it got cold. Madam Vorkinnick delivered another tray of cookies, fresh from the stove and steaming slightly, smiling as she took the empty tray away.

"I've called in some favors," Grodray hung up and walked back over to grab a cookie and stuff it into his mouth all at once. Then he had to drink some coffee before he could speak again.

Eveth's face as she watched was a masterpiece of sarcastic tolerance that nearly made Gareth giggle.

"I've got a few friends being rousted to come here and take over this part of the investigation," Grodray finally managed to speak around the cookies. "Unfortunately, that means we'll have to settle for a pedestrian breakfast elsewhere, instead of whatever Madam Vorkinnick could achieve with a little time to plan. Hopefully it will also make up to the other team for getting up in the middle of the night."

"Where are we going, Jack?" Eveth asked.

"Gareth was right about this being something of a dead end, at least as far as our investigation goes," Grodray smiled at the two of them. "But I do know where we can lay our hands on a pair of experts on wormhole systems at this time of night. We'll grab them, and then head over to a lab and do some thinking."

"Why the hurry?" Eveth asked.

"He has the parts for building two stations, Eve," Grodray said as he grabbed another cookie and held it out like a weapon. "One gets him someplace where nobody could be expected to find him. The other one will bring him back when he's damned good and ready. We have to hunt him now."

"Where's he gone?" Gareth asked anyway, knowing in his soul what the answer was.

"*Earth*," Grodray replied. "Chaa help us when he decides to return."

EXPERT

IF IT HAD BEEN anybody but Xiomber waking him up, Morty might have gone ahead and bitten them. As it was, he still considered it.

"I don't care how good your dream was, you lazy bum," Xiomber grabbed the blankets and pulled them away before Morty could get a good grip and stop him. "Get your sorry ass up."

Morty grumbled a range of profanities at his egg brother and sat up in bed.

"What?" he demanded brusquely.

"Grodray just put in a call and they're headed over here to grab us," Xiomber said. "You got just enough time to shower and get dressed. They said they're taking us to breakfast."

Morty spun and put his socked feet on the floor beside the bed. He had learned to sleep in socks, since the floor tiles in here were always so damned cold, even on a hot day. He ran a hand down his snout, as if that would wipe away whatever silliness had gotten into his brother.

"Fine. I'm up," he groused, standing and stretching. Stripping off his pajamas, he grabbed a towel and headed towards the head.

There was a female Nari officer in the main room. Tonight's jailer, perhaps. She blinked in surprise at the naked Yuudixtl walking by her in socks, but remained silent.

Good for her. If they didn't want to see me naked, they should have let me sleep in.

Behind him, somebody wolf-whistled. Morty turned with a scowl and began to blush furiously at Talyarkinash's grin, as she stood next to the officer.

Women.

He sauntered into the bathroom, wiggling his stubby tail just a little extra as he did, listening to the quiet murmurs and giggles from the two Nari women until the door closed.

Clean, warm, and dressed, he and his brother met Talyarkinash downstairs as a small truck landed in the quad. The sun was about an hour from even starting to brighten the eastern sky, which didn't help his mood.

It was one thing to still be awake to watch the sunrise, after a night of partying and dancing. It was something entirely unnatural to get up and start your day this early.

"Let's move it, cute butt," Talyarkinash said as he stomped down the stairs.

Morty fixed her with a hard, deadly glare, but she seemed to be as utterly immune as most women.

Grumble.

Inside the vehicle, Morty allowed himself to be slightly mollified by freshly baked cookies. Trust those bastards to stop at a coffee shop before getting him, but Grodray had promised food.

Better be good, whatever the hell he thought was worth all this stupidity.

I'm doing my penance here, copper. You don't have to rub my face in it.

Grodray smiled and held out the tray, so Morty took a second cookie.

Okay, maybe.

"Last night, we raided someone you might have dealt with behind some middleman," Grodray said to the two of them. "The name Elnon Ruaidhrí mean anything to you?"

"Art collector?" Xiomber piped up.

"That's right," Grodray said. "He also sold Maximus two, complete wormhole stations worth of equipment, about a month ago."

"Two?" Xiomber asked. "What the hell does he need two for?"

Morty muttered something under his breath, but apparently not far enough under. Talyarkinash's ears and whiskers came forward and then flashed backwards in embarrassment.

"We were right, egg brother," Morty said. "Bastard's going to *Earth* for help."

"That's my theory as well," Grodray said. "From here, we're going to feed you two breakfast, and then head to a secret research facility the Constabulary keeps. Once there, we'll put you two to work."

"How long has he had the equipment?" Morty demanded in a quiet, fierce tone.

"Eleven days from the last shipment," Gareth spoke up.

"Okay, skip breakfast," Morty said. "We need to

head to your lab right now. You can get some pizza delivered, or something, but that's enough time to build and tune one, and use it. That means he's probably already on *Earth*, looking for more killers like him."

"Or worse," Gareth spoke up.

"What could be worse than a hundred Sarzynski's in the *Accord*?" Grodray demanded.

"An entire planet of xenocidal humans finding out that aliens exist, Jack," Baker broke her silence.

Morty nodded to her.

"Finding someone like Maximus wasn't that hard the first time," Morty said. "There is a whole, damned star system filled with people we could have picked from. It was far harder finding Gareth, because there weren't that many heroes, when we went looking."

"Can you find Maximus again?" Baker demanded.

"We can try, Constable," Morty said. "Shouldn't be that hard, since they only have one tube station to look for."

"Then I have news," Grodray said suddenly to the three of them. "It cannot leave this vehicle, or you most likely will be put to death for leaking it. Is that understood?"

Morty watched Talyarkinash nod sharply. Then Xiomber. He was already looking at the walls around him for the rest of his life, so Grodray only had a partial threat. But the Senior Constable was also deadly serious in ways he hadn't even been when he walked into Morty's cell that first time.

"I'm in," Morty said.

"Probably as a result of your meddling, even with

the good you have done, bad things have transpired on *Earth* since Gareth left," Grodray said. "Again, highest level security clearance there is, but you need to know going in, because it will change your equations."

"What the hell has happened?" Gareth demanded, blushing at the profanity that snuck out.

"A human scientist has managed to build his own wormhole generator," Grodray said. "Without our help, or Sarzynski's. It's tiny and short-range right now, but that's a just a matter of time. Especially if they come to realize that we aren't all that far away from them, as far as physics go."

"Crap," Xiomber murmured. "Humans breaking out?"

"Indeed," Grodray agreed. "We have to stop Maximus immediately, but we'll also have to figure out how to stop the humans from finding us. Or finding out about us."

Morty sighed heavily.

Had he really saved the *Accord of Souls* for only a couple of years, just to have Maximus return, at the head of a human army? Was there any, possible, worse outcome?

FIRST INSPECTOR

ANEN WARDSON REVIEWED the preliminary report filed by Prime Investigator Jackeith Grodray with something approximating existential terror. Just a quick note, but more than enough. She had to agree with him that the chances of a human invasion had suddenly gone from merely theoretical to horrifically realistic.

If Maximus had returned home to gather a plague of humans, then it was incumbent upon the First Inspector to protect the *Accord of Souls* at whatever personal or moral cost. She could turn into the worst murderer in history, if the outcome saved an untold future trillions from the sorts of savage death promised by the arrival of humans.

Anen put the document down and let everything inside her chest go for a moment, just because the tension was threatening to make her heart explode out of her chest. She had not gotten to this position by allowing her nerves to get the better of her, but nobody had ever faced a threat so terrible in the fifty thousand years since the Chaa departed, leaving the Vanir to protect the rest of civilization.

She picked up the handset nearby and dialed.

Commissioner Diazal answered quickly.

"How may I be of service, First Inspector?" he asked brightly.

Anen let the dread into her voice finally.

"I have a report from the field, Commissioner," she said. "I would highly recommend that the entire Commission be brought into emergency session, so that I might make a presentation and they can then decide the fate of the galaxy."

She heard the man's sharp intake of breath, but otherwise there was silence on the line for several seconds.

"That bad?" he finally whispered.

"Perhaps worse," she replied. "You and I are removed from the agents in the field, who are removed from the crime, but we may be facing the worst possible scenario my people have been able to think up. Possibly, though the reality maybe be even more terrible."

"We will need an hour to gather the Commissioners on planet," he said. "I will send messengers after the others, but we may have a quorum at hand. How long do we have?"

"I do not know, Commissioner," she said. "But we are facing the potential of an imminent, human invasion."

FISHERMAN

GARETH HAD NEVER ACTUALLY SEEN what a tube station looked like. He had only ever passed through the tubes themselves. And most stations were largely automated to the extent that an engineer pressed a button and perhaps slid a level to open and scale a tube, depending on traffic.

This thing in front of him wasn't quite home-brewed, but it had the appearance of something put together by a hobbyist, rather than purpose built.

"Where the hell did you confiscate this?" Morty asked as he followed Gareth into the room.

Xiomber was a step behind him, and the two Yuudixtl politely hip-checked the Vanir Constable who had been standing there out of their way. That their heads came up to the man's thigh didn't intimidate those two one bit.

Gareth stepped into a handy corner out of the way, with Talyarkinash standing close. Eveth and Jackeith followed Morty and Xiomber.

The machine looked like nothing so much as

antique images Gareth had seen of a musical recording studio, where a sound engineer could individually control hundreds of settings with petite, vertical sliders, until he had the exact sound he wanted. Dozens of larger dials ran across the top, with needles next to them as you adjusted.

"You don't think we built the machine?" Grodray replied bluntly to the Yuudixtl as he got close.

"No," Xiomber said with a definite sneer. "You'd have ordered all the same parts ahead of time. This was whatever someone could find in every pawnshop and junkyard they knew."

Gareth had to agree with that. On closer examination, everything was slightly different as he went down the line. It was like someone had added the first slider, and then gone looking for the second, affixing it before they went for the third.

"Hey," the Constable scientist snapped as Morty began making adjustments, "You aren't supposed to touch that."

"Grodray, make him go away," Morty said flatly. "Xiomber and I can't work with mother hen here making noise."

"I beg your pardon?" the man started to get angry. At least until Grodray turned to him and sent him from the room with a head toss. The man departed, grumbling under his breath. Gareth assumed he was going as far as the next room, behind a mirror that looked two-way from the long angle Gareth had to watch.

"Also, cops wouldn't tune it like this," Xiomber turned his head and gestured at the row of dials and needle gauges. "This looks like a cat burglar rig."

"What's that?" Grodray asked.

Gareth couldn't tell if the question was honest or just humoring the two lizards.

"One man in, but the far tunnel entrance is soft," Morty said louder. "So the tube stays open, and someone can just chuck things into the tube from the far end and they'll come out here. Ya gotta be quick, since most security systems will scream bloody murder as soon as they detect the intrusion, but you still have maybe eighty seconds, depending on where a guard is."

"You've done this sort of thing before," Grodray accused him.

"We've been convicted of it, Grodray," Morty snapped. "Remember? Pages three, eleven, and fourteen of the grand indictment, in case you've forgotten."

Grodray fell silent as the two began running their hands over everything. Gareth noted that they didn't make any adjustments, at least not yet. More just familiarization, with sounds of happiness emerging from the two.

"Burritos or pizza?" Morty asked out of the blue.

"Burritos for breakfast," Xiomber decided. "We can get pizzas send over later."

Morty turned to Grodray and Baker.

"Four breakfast burritos, please," he even sounded remarkably polite. "Two extra spicy. Two with extra sour cream. Lots of meat and cheese."

Baker nodded and departed while the rest of them watched.

"Now what?" Gareth asked in a quiet tone as Grodray stepped close to them.

Grodray, at least, seemed satisfied with things for now.

"Now I play a hunch," the man replied. "Challenge their professional credentials to find the man and figure out if we need to send a team through or if we can just grab Maximus and his gang and drag them to justice."

"How long do we have?" Gareth asked. "I know you filed reports with your bosses. What will they do?"

"Right now, Gareth?" Grodray's voice fell so quiet that Gareth and Talyarkinash had to lean in to follow. "Right now, they may be deciding to destroy Earth if we can't stop Maximus before he does whatever it is he had planned."

Gareth felt the spike of cold adrenaline land at the pit of his stomach.

Pippa. Dr. Loughty. All of his friends in Sky Patrol. All of Earth Force.

All of Earth.

All of humanity might be doomed because of Marc Sarzynski's rage. And there was nothing he could do about it, except rely on a pair of semi-reformed, career criminals, and the very Constabulary that might decide to wipe out his entire species.

GENERAL

MARC WALKED BACK into the main chamber, holding the pocketcomm he had taken from the mob boss.

"Anything?" Zorge asked, looking up from a small piece of equipment he had been tinkering on, in the middle of the poker table.

"Maybe," Marc replied, reaching for the Vanir-sized table he had brought over and settling into it.

Maiair had been making tea. Yooyar had apparently been standing nearby her sister. Both drifted his way and took up the other two chairs. The three androids stood guard, and Mishalska had been left asleep on a cot in the garage for now.

Marc turned to check, but the three doors holding the six mobsters were closed. Locked from this side by some gadgets Zorge had brought.

"I was able to reach some of my old contacts," Marc continued. "Problem is, most of them got rolled up by Gareth Dankworth and Sky Patrol over the last two years when I disappeared. Several of the people I talked to suggested ever so vaguely that I had been caught by the cops, turned, and was now in the process of setting them up."

"Ouch," Zorge commiserated. "Where does that leave us?"

"I've got a couple of other places to look for help," Marc's smile gained wattage. "People like Cleveland Eddy and Two-Gun Kowalski are doing long stretches in federal penitentiaries right now. I just need to figure out which ones, and then we'll bust them out."

"Huh? Oh, right," Zorge snapped his fingers. "I'm not used to living in a place that doesn't have wormhole alarms everywhere. Will they even know what happened?"

"No," Marc turned serious. "The jailers will just discover them gone one morning, from a locked cell, with no indication how it happened. Better will be if they have life-monitors going, and both just go blank on the tape."

"Ya know, I could get to liking this place," Zorge said with a smile.

"What about the current prisoners?" Maiair asked, sipping her tea.

"Two of the grunts look like they'll play," Marc said. "O'Rourke might be a harder nut to crack, at least until Two-Gun walks in here and smiles at him."

"Why would that matter?" Yooyar asked, perking up.

"The man has a scar running from chin to hairline on the left side," Marc said. "Looks like an old,

Prussian, dueling scar, but it was done by a razor blade when he was a teenager. Mob boss didn't like the kid smiling at the man's daughter, so he cut him."

"Really?" Maiair was shocked. "Did it scare him off?"

"Oh no," Marc laughed. "Two-Gun stalked the man and killed him later. Cut his body into pieces and left them in a pile on the man's front stoop. One of the two guns he got famous for later was taken from the guy. He's a real piece of work, but we go way back and he'll be grateful to be sprung."

"What about the rest?" Yooyar asked.

"I'll work on them some more, but we may just end up killing them afterwards to keep them quiet," Marc said. "Can't turn them loose right now, or they'll lead the cops right to us, most likely. And I need this place as a base for the station, at least until we can move it all somewhere else. And to do that, I need human agents who can take out a lease and things like that. Most of it can be done electronically these days, but I don't exist right now, and the machines responsible will balk if I tried."

"How hard are the machines to hack?" Zorge perked up. Nothing like a challenge to keep his head in the game.

"Child's play, compared to the *Accord*," Marc replied. "We've only had computers for about three centuries at this point, and Artificial Intelligence is still just a really complicated decision tree flipping coins."

"So get me access to a trunk and we can do something about that," Zorge nodded.

"Not quite as easy as walking into a café and

connecting to their channel," Marc said. "Well, technically, that's not true. It is that easy. It's the getting out again afterwards that presents a problem. At least for a Nari or a Warreth or a Vanir."

"And thus, Cleveland Eddy and Two-Gun," Maiair completed the thought.

"Exactly," Marc agreed. "How soon to get everything set up and calibrated?"

Zorge shrugged, leaning back in his chair and letting his eyes focus on a distant horizon. He scratched the whiskers on the right side of his chin for a moment.

"Since we don't need to go off planet for the first jump, probably about a week or tenday," Zorge said. "I can refine things much tighter after that. How many people were you wanting to bring here?"

"Just those two, for now," Marc said. "Then maybe some members of my old gang that Gareth caught on that last day, if we can track them down. That gives us humans we can use as front men for the rest of things. Men who can't turn us in to the cops without going down themselves."

"Gotcha, boss," Zorge said. "Time to rouse the kid and get to work."

Rather than say anything more, he rose and headed towards the garage, where much of the equipment had been stored next to a late-model truck that had been converted to a limousine for O'Rourke and his gang.

Yooyar surprised Marc by joining the old Nari, leaving him alone with Maiair.

"We'll also need to set out to find you a wife," Maiair said quietly, placing one hand on his arm gently.

"That can wait," Marc replied. "We'll have years, if everything goes according to plan. I didn't really know any good candidates before, when I was a cop. Well, I did, but they're the kind that like cops."

"I know," she smiled. "We'll need to find you one like Liamssen. That will be my job, since she's going to have to measure up to my standards, if I expect her to keep you entertained."

Marc smiled back wanly. It was odd, falling into this sort of role, somewhere between Bonaparte and a Pasha from a fairy tale with a harem of beautiful women.

But she was right. Whoever they found would have to have a first-rate mind, on top of legendary beauty. That kid O'Rourke had brought had been attractive enough, until the moment she opened her screachy mouth.

She had at least gotten over her screaming fits, but Marc was pretty sure he'd had better and more rewarding conversations with house cats.

One step at a time. As she had said. Make Earth safe. Then recruit an army and take it over to conquer the *Accord of Souls*. Only then would he be able to come back and conquer his homeworld.

Humans were just too fractious a people. He knew that. But with *Accord* technology and an army composed of Vanir, Nari, and the rest that had broken to his will, he could keep his boot on humanity's throat.

At that point, the only problem would be the first three or four humans who tried to do the same thing to him, raising a human army on a crusade against evil and aliens.

Because only humans would fight other humans hard enough.

Still, Emperor Marc, Conqueror of the Universe.

Yes, that would do.

COMMISSION

ANEN STOOD before the body that represented the very *Accord of Souls* itself, wondering if she also faced the apocalypse.

Commissioner Diazal had managed to located eight of the others. That was more than a quorum. It was slightly over half of the worthies that sat on that body.

They had convened in strictest secrecy. Nobody else was allowed in the room, not even aides. although she had no doubts that it was being recorded and would eventually leak out. However, unlike most leaks, this one would potentially subject even an *Accord Commissioner* to life imprisonment. They would, at least, be careful.

For now, it was just important that the dangerous scope of things be abundantly clear.

Anen stood below the Commissioners on their raised, curved platform that allowed each to see one another and to surround whoever came before them.

Petim Diazal rose from his seat, next to the empty

one where the Proctor would have sat, save for being on vacation this week, where a message was even now chasing after the man. In his stead, Diazal was discretely exercising executive authority. He would do that anyway, in another year or so, when the current Proctor finally retired after a lifetime of glorious service.

"Comrades," Diazal began in a serious voice, drawing all eyes to him magnetically. "I have been informed of a serious threat to the very *Accord of Souls* that we have all sworn to uphold and protect. As many of you are aware, I have been working with the First Inspector on an enquiry regarding the criminal known as Maximus. In the last fourteen hours, we have had a sudden escalation so critical that it became necessary to convene in Emergency Council, and perhaps make permanent, binding decisions. Our other Commissioners have had messengers sent to them, and will be joining us as soon as they can, but it may not be possible to wait even that long."

He paused there, hanging the room on pins and needles as he looked at each of the other faces, and the empty chairs. Finally, he turned his attention to her.

"First Inspector Wardson," he said simply. "Could you please bring the rest of the Commission up to date on the things you have previously told me?"

Anen studied all of those faces in turn. Most were friendly. A few dubious, but that was a personality trait on their part, and not hostility to her or the Constabulary. The crimes uncovered by Jack and Eve over the last year had been made abundantly clear to everyone.

The Commission was clean. Several members of the House of Worlds, on the other hand, had been arrested once all the evidence came out.

They would be a decade or more cleaning up this mess, but because of her people, and even a Star Dragon, they would have that time, rather than falling beneath the heel of a tyrant. She hoped.

"Commissioners of the *Accord of Souls*," Anen began. "We have been pursuing the criminal known as Maximus for over a year now. While he had managed to elude us on several occasions, his criminal brethren have not been so lucky, and the Constabulary has struck many telling blows against a criminal underworld whose scope had been previously unimaginable."

Many heads nodded. Everyone had been rather aghast at how badly corrupt other politicians had become.

"Recently, we have broken yet another criminal ring," Anen continued. "In the process, we have discovered that Maximus has in his control all the necessary components to build himself two, complete wormhole tube stations. He has escaped us again, but we have a scenario we are pursuing."

"At what point, madam, does this require emergency action on our part?" the Enjev Commissioner, Q'quivk'k spoke up. "As you have stated previously, you continue to hound him. Is it not just a matter of time until the criminal is in custody?"

Enjev were a bipedal species uplifted from something like an arachnid originally. Four major limbs, like a Vanir, plus two more, delicate arms mid-torso. Their mandibles gave little clue as to their thinking, unlike a Vanir's face, so you had to watch the four hands for unspoken cues. Q'quivk'k's body hair was blue-gray not that far removed from Anen's uniform, and beginning to age into the golden-yellow of his final stage.

"It is, Commissioner Q'quivk'k," Anen replied, keeping her tone under control. He wasn't an enemy. Just a sharp politician looking for an edge he could dangle over her. "However, it is the primary theory of my investigators in the field that Maximus has built one station and used it to flee someplace where he can hide from us for a very long time, while he puts in place a true threat to the *Accord.*"

"Which would be?" the Commissioner nearly sneered at her.

"Recruiting a human army, with which he will return and attempt to conquer the entire *Accord of Souls,*" she said flatly. Might as well brush the Commissioner's verbal games completely aside at the beginning, rather than fence with him all night.

That certainly got everyone's attention. It took Petim several minutes to get everything back under control from the various outbursts and howling.

"My apologies, First Inspector," Petim said as he finally got everyone to shut up. "Could you please give us a cursory background that brings us up to the current?"

"Why is that necessary?" Q'quivk'k's demanded. "Why not simply drop a force on Earth and arrest Maximus?"

"Because we don't know exactly where he is," Anen spoke before anyone else could. "We are searching, but there are ten billion humans in that system we must identify. It will take time we may not have."

"And what's your worst-case response, First Inspector?" Q'quivk'k's voice turned grim and dark now.

"I have spoken with Commissioner Diazal about the possibility of using a bio-weapon to end all human life, wherever it might be found in their entire home system," she replied, even more harshly. "We cannot wait until they break out, and only then attempt to inoculate our worlds, because something that virulent will no doubt begin to mutate with time, and might become a threat to the Vanir, or the Nari. Or the Enjev, Commissioner."

If the first outburst had been manic, this one was truly apocalyptic. Everyone was yelling, crying, demanding, pounding tables, threatening. Everyone except Q'quivk'k. Hs just sat and watched Anen. She returned a cold smile.

The Commissioner nodded once, and rose.

Q'quivk'k slammed his upper right hand into the table top like a gunshot. Everyone fell to silence in shock, as that Commissioner was normally a placid, quiet type.

Q'quivk'k turned to his right.

"Commissioner Diazal, my apologies for the outburst," he said in a polite tone before turning back to her. "First Inspector, what else do we need to know?"

Anen told them, watching faces grow pale as she did.

ROCKER

AS TRAPS WENT, Royston had been in worse and survived. Of course, those were just threats to his body. Tonight was about his soul. Or at least his intellectual reputation.

They had been waiting in a coffee shop not far from the British Library, he site of today's sightseeing. Pippa was dressed in green, and Fatima wore an abaya wrap the color of golden sand, with a blue hijab, both in silk, that she had bought at a local tailor who specialized in Muslim fashion.

It still made Royston's breath catch, watching her drink her tea and smile at him.

Two men walked in. Most of the customers in here barely noticed them walk up to the counter and order, but Royston had been a Sky Patrol agent when he was their age. Before science took over his life.

He recognized the way the men walked, if not the faces.

They got their coffee and retired to a table nearby,

one watching the doors and the other the kitchen and the restrooms.

Royal Special Services.

"Our friend should arrive in approximately four minutes," Royston murmured to the two women.

Pippa looked perplexed, but Fatima fixed him with sharp eyes.

"The two men who just walked in?" she asked simply.

Royston nodded and sipped his coffee mildly.

Right on time, Prince Henry walked in, looked around, and smiled at them. Quickly, the young man ordered coffee and approached.

Royston found it terribly amusing that the young man had managed a Mod look tonight rather than the more-formal tweeds he had worn the previous two times Royston had met him.

For this evening blue dungarees, a little long and rolled up twice at the ankle, as was the style. Plain, white t-shirt under a black denim jacket. The boy's hair was not long enough to slick back into a large pompadour with a duck tail, but that was the only part that might make him stand out from the expected crowd.

Coffee in hand, Henry joined them. Royston found it amusing that Pippa had to fight the urge to stand in his presence, while he and Fatima sat companionably. Still, the boy was a natural as an actor. He fell into the fourth chair with a hearty grin and sipped his coffee, an innocent joining some older friends for a night of music.

"Good evening," he said. "Thank you for not putting up too much of a struggle with my mother. "

Royston nodded. The Queen could have done this

so much less delicately, but that wasn't her style, either.

"We have about half an hour, Henry," Royston said. "The theater is a little over three blocks from here."

"Please, at least for tonight, call me Hank," the boy implored. "I don't often get to escape the confines of the Palace, where everything must be proper and precise."

"Hank," Pippa tried the name on a bit dubiously.

Two more men entered a few minutes after the prince, taking up the opposite corner from their compatriots and placing Royston and his party in a lovely, little box of safety. He had no doubts that several more men, perhaps a full rifle platoon, were someplace close against need.

Hopefully, nothing would ever come of it.

They made small talk for a time. Hank was interested in Persia, as an exotic location he might never visit, so Fatima was able to talk about her supposed home and show off the extensive research she had done.

Finally, they rose to depart. Considering the evening ahead, Royston had Fatima on his arm, while Pippa took charge of Hank. It helped that the man was so tall, and that his daughter had eyes for nobody but Gareth.

Fatima, in the interests of science, had chosen not to drug her sensory tentacles into quiescence tonight, but darkness on the streets and in the theater would hopefully shelter her from watchers. And nobody would be allowed to get close enough to them on the streets of London to present a threat to the Crown Prince.

Of that, Royston had no doubts whatsoever.

The theatre itself was an old, rundown sort of place. A neighborhood playhouse, when it was originally built, perhaps, with an excellent stage only three feet above the front row, and a well-designed bowl of seats, where everyone would have an unobstructed view of young Hamlet dying in the middle of the space.

The curtain was closed, as that night before. Red velvet as was classical. They had arrived a touch early tonight. Not quite first, but close enough for Royston to have his pick of seats, centered about two third of the way back. It would put him almost on eye level with the woman at the microphone, a necessity Royston didn't understand, but he wasn't willing to dispute his instincts.

Most of the early birds were down front anyway tonight, so Royston ended up with Hank on his right and Fatima on his left, with Pippa guarding the Prince's far side like a hawk. Fatima had kept her arm entwined with his for the whole walk over, and regained it now, once they were seated.

He gave her a questioning look, but she simply leaned her head against his shoulder with a smile, where he could feel her tentacles moving around under her hijab, even through the herringbone of his jacket.

Quickly enough, the room filled, every seat claimed and an extra row of people across the back, where a low wall marked off a small balcony for more folks to watch over their heads. At least four of them had followed the group from the coffee house.

The lights went down, plunging the room into

near-ultimate darkness and a silence so complete Royston could hear the audience breathing.

The curtains peeled apart, revealing the same band as before in just enough light that the musicians could see each other and their instruments. The audience would be a black hole before them.

When he had attended other concerts of a similar ilk, at Henry or Pippa's age, the opening of the curtains was normally a cue for the audience to begin clapping and cheering, but tonight, everything remained utterly silent.

It was as though she had already cast her spell and captured them in her web.

The woman was dressed as before, in turquoise silk dress slashed to her hip and barely covering her to mid-thigh. Opera gloves in black. Black pumps. Her long, brunette hair was wild and loose, billowing lightly in the breeze of a fan at the front of the stage and centered up on her.

Before, she had only spoke at the very end, but tonight she seemed to feel the air of magic about her. She looked out over the darkness that hid the audience and seemed to find Royston with a smile and a tiny nod

"Good to see you again," she said, turning to the drummer with a harder nod, even as Royston's soul went cold with a dread he could not name.

Drums.

Syncopated jazz had a drummer to keep a soft, almost swishing beat, well in the background, against which the rest of the musicians counted.

This man, this *drummer*, was not interested in jazz.

The bass drum started first with a staggered,

double beat. It was the heartbeat of the galaxy itself sounding.

Over it, the drummer began to play the rest of his instrument.

On a piano, a player can stab down the highest key on his right and then run the entire keyboard with the back of his hand, like an avalanche descending to the lowest notes. Doing the exact same thing with a drum set required this man to rotate gymnastically as he played more than twenty drums in sequence.

The effect was the same. The power was uncontrollable.

Bass player next. Upright and calling for the very dead to rise and take the world. Royston found his heart and his feet beating in tune.

The rest of the band joined in, the piano first and then two guitars, followed by a Siren calling all the foolish sailors to their deaths onto the rocks.

If Royston had imagined he had seen all of this woman's power and capabilities before, he was sadly mistaken. Or perhaps she had taken something from him as well, on that night when she gave him the higher physics, because tonight, she had ascended the very heavens and carried several hundred innocent music fans with her.

Royston leaned back to listen. And hopefully survive the onslaught of power embracing them.

As before, she spoke no more. Just a pause between song to tune instruments and drink water, before diving headlong into the next.

Somewhere in the middle, a torch song of love and loneliness. Royston was shocked at his behavior, but it felt perfectly natural to turn and kiss Fatima, and she seemed to feel the same way. They finally broke with a blush, but she did not withdraw. Just rested her head and tentacles on his shoulder again.

A quick glance over, but Hank was utterly enraptured and hadn't noticed. Nor had Pippa, hopefully. He was far too old to be fooling around with an alien secret agent.

The song was over all too soon anyway.

The woman on stage ended her tune with everyone breathless. Rather than close the curtains or take a drink, she looked up in surprise, the entire auditorium seemingly forgotten.

Royston felt it a moment later. Something drew his head to the heavens. And perhaps his soul.

"What is it?" Fatima whispered, but that was a question Royston could not answer.

And then the world ended.

RAIDERS

GARETH KNEW the moment had arrived by the way both Yuuixtl sat up straighter and stared at each other. He was the only other person in the room, the others having retired into the adjoining chamber to watch through the two-way mirror. Just in case, he rapped his knuckles smartly on the glass to get everyone's attention.

Morty and Xiomber had their heads together, murmuring quietly when the rest of the team burst into the room.

"What have you got?" Jackeith demanded.

"I think we've found him," Morty said. "Xiomber's certain, but I'm only rating it four deviations."

"That's a damned, high number," Baker said as she moved with Grodray towards the center of the room.

"Yeah, but multiply it by ten billion and you've still got a lot of other people it might be," Morty snarled back. "Even at this distance, it's a royal pain in the ass narrowing the field down."

"You did it once," Grodray accused. "Twice actually."

He nodded in Gareth's direction as the four of them, three Constabulary and one Nari scientist, hovered over the two Yuudixtl.

"And both times we were looking for an emotional signature," Xiomber snapped. "Cinra wanted a pure killer. Morty wanted a hero. Finding an archetype is a lot easier than finding a person. I can't just program in *Vanir* and have it look. We have to nail down a criminal psyche profile."

"Really?" Grodray seemed unconvinced.

"You got any idea how many criminals there are on Earth, copper?" Morty snarled.

"I do," Gareth spoke up to defuse them before emotions got out of control.

It was just the stress talking now. The risk that they were so far behind Marc that he would have time to raise an entire army of killers ready to come over and destroy the *Accord of Souls.*

Still, everyone paused, turning to Gareth.

"I was Sky Patrol," Gareth said. "Am Sky Patrol. My entire career has been dedicated to fighting crime. The few times I got to rescue maidens from something other than dragons I could probably count on one hand. If you think the Constabulary has had a hard time lately, multiply that by the centuries my kind have been trying to keep a lid on things here without the psionic resonance of the *Accord.*"

He fixed Baker and Grodray with a hard look.

"There's one way to do this," he said. "Someone has to go through and determine."

"No," Grodray said. "If one person goes through, we have to send an entire team, otherwise one person might get killed before they can report back. At best, this tips Maximus off and he runs. At worse, it starts a war."

"And a whole assault force won't?" Gareth asked.

"If it does, it will be on our terms," Grodray replied. He turned to Morty. "Safe enough bet to scare the hell out of a group of innocents if we land on them?"

"Ain't nobody innocent where I'm going to drop you, Grodray," Morty said. "Maybe not Maximus when you get there, but it isn't the same thing as they don't have it coming. Personally, I'd take disintegrators instead of stunners, and just kill the lot of them, but I have a low opinion of someone that scores this high on the psychopath scale in the first place. Plus, he might have more of those android things that nearly kicked Gareth's ass last time."

Grodray was in command, so everyone waited for his decision.

"Talus, you listening?" Grodray asked out loud.

"I am," the Senior Constable in charge of the facility answered over the speakers.

"Alert One," Grodray said. "Get my team in motion and gear. Have local security teams ready to step in here, in case someone comes back through the tube other than us. I'll send a note to the First Inspector. Everyone has one hour to drop. Plan accordingly and meet here in full assault gear."

The room exploded into motion. Gareth followed Grodray and Baker to the suite where their rooms were in order to arm himself. Like the previous missions, stunner and heavy disintegrator pistols went into the holsters. They would do the same. The rest of the team would have both, but most likely keep the disintegrator holstered until necessary.

Gareth could shoot with both hands, as could Eve and Jack.

He didn't eat, knowing that the adrenaline would sour anything in his stomach, but Gareth did settle for a mug of honey-laden coffee to pep himself up without being so acidic that it curdled on him. He had to assume Marc would be waiting for them on the other side of the tube, probably firing as soon as he had a target.

Hopefully, they could flood the far end with enough guns and shooters to clear the room out, if it came to that.

Back at the staging area, he was surprised when Talyarkinash joined them, dressed for the field and with a bag slung over her shoulder.

"What do you think you are doing, Dr. Liamssen?" Grodray demanded in a low voice.

"You'll need a second medic with you," she said simply. "You only have one right now, and if something happens to him, you'll have none. I'm a fully licensed doctor, so I can join you as a field medic. Plus, I've been there since damned near the beginning, so I claim the right to be there at the end."

"You might get killed, Liamssen," Baker tried to dissuade her.

Gareth nearly laughed. Talyarkinash was at least as stubborn as the two Vanir.

At least.

"And Maximus might have killed me several times over, Baker," Talyarkinash snapped back at the woman. "He didn't stick a knife in your arm. Or offer to slice your throat. Keep that in mind."

Every eye turned to Grodray now. He studied the group closely. In the background, fifteen more troopers were filing in and lining up along the walls, but they remained silent in their field armor and firepower.

"On your head. Liamssen," Grodray finally decided. But he nodded.

"I would not have it any other way, Grodray," Talyarkinash replied.

Gareth turned to the two Yuudixtl scientists.

"Morty, will this tube hold a dragon?" he asked.

"Sure, kid," Morty said. "But this room's barely big enough just for you. And I got no idea of the space I'm dropping you, except that it's a room of some size. Wouldn't do it until you got there, just to be sure."

"Understood," Gareth said.

He could chance it. Transform into the Star Dragon in the middle of the transit and arrive at the other end in his great form.

But it was risky. He might come out in a place too small to maneuver. On the other hand, if he came out in his Vanir form, it would cost him several seconds to transform, possibly while a firefight was happening.

"Scout first, Gareth," Grodray ordered him. "You, Baker, then me into the tunnel. My team after that. Then Dr. Liamssen. If necessary, we'll hold them off long enough for you to change."

"Understood, sir," Gareth said.

He moved to a spot in front of the others, along

the far part of the room where Morty and Xiomber would open a tunnel to *Earth*.

"Everybody set?" Xiomber called out across the rustling of bodies.

The noise fell to silence. Gareth drew both pistols and prepared to confront the man who had once been his closest friend in the world.

"Now," Grodray said simply.

Morty nodded and began shifting levers.

The generators behind the machine were in a separate part of the facility, so they weren't close enough to hear. At least not unless one of them exploded.

Still, the lights flickered under the enormous drain. They would be putting twenty bodies through a small generator station, rather than one of the big, industrial units for transporting vehicles. But those were permanently locked to a single tube and optimized.

Building this sort of apparatus required you to be able to target any point in the galaxy and lock onto it. And this unit had been home built from scratch by some criminal genius. It began to hum ominously as it drew power into itself. Not loud, but an unpleasant snarl of energy rather like a hive of angry wasps about to emerge.

"Grodray, we are go," Morty yelled over the noise.

"Open the tube," the Senior Constable, the Prime Investigator in disguise, ordered.

Gareth watched a Yuudixtl hand grab the big level on the end and push it all the way to the stops. In front of him, gold began to form in the very air.

He flashed back to leaving Earth the first time,

under the control of those same two men. It felt right that they were the ones sending him back now, however temporary this mission would be.

At least he would be on *Earth* one last time in his life.

The portal opened. Gareth felt the softest breeze come over his shoulders and enter, like a whirlpool seeking to drown sailors.

"All weapons off safety and ready to engage," Grodray ordered the room.

They were going in hot. It was the only way to be sure.

"Gareth, into the tube," came the call.

Gareth stepped forward and felt the universe unravel around him as the tunnel took hold.

Last time, it had been frightening. Now, he felt nothing but anger.

He was going to kill Marc. Nothing short of that would ever make the galaxy safe. It saddened Gareth, but this was the moment when the greater needs of the trillions of being alive and yet to be born outweighed a handful of fools intent on upsetting the apple cart.

He took a deep breath, unsure how long it would take to arrive. He would need to land, scan the entire room, and probably open fire in an eyeblink. Or at least draw fire to him so that Baker and Grodray could get the drop on whoever was shooting. Hopefully, nothing but pistols shooting hot lead. His field armor would offer some protection.

A heavy disintegrator, like the one in his left hand, would just cut him in half.

Gareth felt his heartbeat surging, pounding in his chest and his ears.

The tunnel suddenly grew cold around him, rather than the normal warmth it conveyed.

Gareth felt a moment of panic as it felt like he was slowing down.

Was that even possible?

And then his entire universe lit up with white fire.

APOCALYPSE

IT HAD TAKEN TWO DAYS, but Marc figured that Two-Gun was finally starting to calm down. He didn't twitch every time he saw a Warreth female or a Nari male. The three androids had barely bothered him a bit.

"You ready to finally talk?" Marc asked.

The two of them were sitting at the poker table, sipping coffee. Zorge and Mishalska were in the garage, tuning the machine to make longer tubes. Maiair and Yooyar were over on the kitchenette side of the space, pointedly keeping a polite distance.

Two-Gun set his coffee down and stared up at Marc.

"It feels like some bizarre Halloween thing," he said in a surprisingly high tenor voice. He was a tall man, six two, but lanky and fast. The scar on his face made him look hideous, but the rest of him had once been pretty enough for the girls to swoon over.

"I understand," Marc said. "Over there, humans

are unknown demons that mothers threaten their children with. I had to take on a Vanir form in order to hide."

"You planning to do that to me?" Two-Gun asked nervously.

"Not now," Marc said. "Maybe later, if you decide you want to. We might be able to erase the scar when we did, but I can't promise anything until I talk to a geneticist."

"It's all right for now," Two-Gun said. "Been this way for fifteen years. Not sure I'd like looking at myself in the mirror without it. Or with the ears."

"Changing form takes some getting used to," Marc agreed. "At least for me it did."

"So you sprung me from prison," the shooter said. "What's the play?"

"I've got gold and some first-class forged paper bills and identity papers," Marc said. "You'll go into civilization in O'Roark's vehicle and set yourself up with a bank account and such. I think Seattle's a safer bet than the East Coast. They ignore outsiders up there, so you'll be able to work. Rent yourself a flat and find us a warehouse to move all our equipment to. Then rent a big truck and drive it back out here. We dismantle everything, pack it to wherever you landed, and set up again. From there, we build an army."

"Ya know, Portland's even smaller and more insular than Seattle," Two-Gun offered.

"True, but it's also a surprisingly racist town, even today," Marc countered. "After the way they treat non-WASPs, could you imagine the reaction to a Nari or a Warreth? At least a Vanir could be passed off as a human from a distance. No, Seattle doesn't really care what color or shape you are, as long as you have money."

"Gotcha, boss," Two-Gun said. "And you'll just trust me with money and a new identity? No chaperone? Nothing?"

"It's not like I can't find you if I wanted to," Marc threatened the man politely. "And you're back in the pen in a heartbeat if someone does recognize you, so you need someplace safe to hide as bad as I do. I can offer you the entire galaxy to vanish into. At least until we conquer Earth and you're no longer a fugitive."

That brought a rough smile.

"Sound good," he said. "When do I depart."

"Probably…"

Zorge came blasting through the door to the garage with a beam pistol in his hand and wild look in his eyes.

"Tube warning," he yelled as he found a spot with cover and dropped in. "Someone's coming through!"

Marc grabbed the table and carried it towards a side wall. It wouldn't stop much, but it would hide him for a second.

"Two-Gun, this way," he yelled, drawing the small human in his wake.

Around the room, Maiair and Yooyar also drew weapons, as did the three androids.

As armed laagers went, not much, but hopefully good enough. All he could offer right now was a rabid porcupine.

Marc felt the tube begin to take shape. The air

tasted golden and warm over in one corner, where someone was about to drop Constables on him.

We'll just have to see about that.

And then the world ended.

THE COMMUNION

"HAVE ALL ARRIVED?" a voice asked the darkness.

"We are come, *Speaker for the Communion*," another voice answered.

Speaker for the Communion looked out and counted the sigils around him. Twelve, as in ancient times, when the last council of the Chaa voted to ascend to godhead. Even *Seeker for the Knee of God* was here, brought by no less than *First Immortal* herself, the two farthest wanderers having come home for the first time in a Chitra or more.

"I call *The Communion* to witness," he said to the other minds. "The vote to include the humans in the past was just and clear. The *Accord of Souls* was shaped without them, and has remained. But all of our expectations of human cultural development have proven inaccurate to a degree that requires a return to the original Plan. *Docent*, you would speak?"

"All such plans are estimates," the *Great Teacher* replied mildly. "Five Chitra is a long time in the life span of any species unmodified. Wrong conveys value. We cannot know God's plan without asking It."

"So noted," *Speaker for the Communion* said. "*Last Traveler*, how great is the danger?"

"When I first tasted the signs, the risk was measured in centuries," the most compassionate said. "However, look ye now and absorb the essence of change about to unfold around us."

Speaker for the Communion felt the sigils of two of his kin engulf this world of humans and draw forth the indications. One was *Glory in Sunrise*, named for the happiness in exploration for no greater reason than learning and seeing.

The other had been her brother, once upon a time incarnated. He had been called *Bowsprit* then, as the foremost point of the Ship of Heaven, but his sigil had grown inward, complicated over the Chitra. It might best be enunciated as *Astray in Darkness* today, indicating one that has gone deeper into the wilds and not yet found the way out.

Perhaps *The Communion* would need to assist.

"*Last Traveler* speaks truth," *Glory in Sunrise* spoke for her brother. "The risk is imminent, even on corporeal scales. We must act."

"I call *The Communion* to *Almar*," another voice broke in.

Speaker for the Communion joined the others in returning to the very soil from which they once departed, five Chitra ago.

"So," *Narrator of History* spoke now. "Our grandchildren have spoken for war on the humans of their own volition. They will wipe out the species in defensive terror. What says *The Communion*?"

"I will not allow it," *Merciless* spoke, breaking the silence of nearly a Chitra. "I must already stand one day before God for such a crime. No others should have to stand with me."

"Will you accept responsibility for a second expunging?" *Speaker for the Communion* asked, taking the taste of the minds about him.

"I will."

"Who else would speak?"

"We move in undue haste," *First Immortal* suddenly dominated them with her sigil. "It is true that we might have moments until such war breaks out, but it is acted upon in ignorance of *The Great Plan*. Of *The Communion*. Humans have no understanding that other species even exist as yet. We must judge them accordingly, but we must reveal ourselves to them first."

"And if they will not bow?" *The Mountain* asked.

"*The Communion* is already gathered," she replied. "We can summon the entire *Ascended Chaa* and place this vote before such a congress."

Speaker for the Communion noted the votes of his fellows and saw the way forward. Looking outward, he saw the terrified leaders of *Almar* preparing a crude biological weapon to unleash on the humans. He noted Constables of the *Accord of Souls* already in motion to kill or be killed, attempting to arrest the creature at the core of the troubles.

One such Constable stood out.

The creature wore the form of a Vanir, but was not of the *Accord*. He was human in a second guise. With a third contained within.

Most interesting. The human was capable of a higher form.

Perhaps they had chosen well, seven Chitra ago when they left the humans to develop. Such creatures might yet *Ascend*, if a Star Dragon was any clue.

But time was measured in seconds now.

The war was already begun. Only the Chaa could end it. Should end it.

Their own failures had brought the galaxy thus.

He reached out a hand and stopped time itself.

Humans acted in ignorance, it was true, but their crimes were no less savage for it. They would be placed on trial. The entire *Communion* would judge.

Speaker for the Communion caused his voice to emerge from every speaker device in the entire *Accord of Souls*, and every room on *Earth*, regardless of technology. He intercepted every wormhole traversing into or out of Earth and prevented the Commissioners on *Almar* from opening a new one to destroy the humans with their weapon.

Finally, he gathered up all of the souls responsible for the current state of affairs, including several humans who had no inkling of the coming role they would play.

"PEOPLE OF THE EARTH, YOU WILL HEAR ME."

READ MORE!

Be sure to read all of the Star Dragon books!

Birth of the Star Dragon
Flight of the Star Dragon
Call of the Star Dragon
Shadow of the Star Dragon
Trial of the Star Dragon

ABOUT THE AUTHOR

Blaze Ward writes science fiction in the Alexandria Station universe (Jessica Keller, The Science Officer, The Story Road, etc.) as well as several other science fiction universes, such as Star Dragon, the Collective, and more. He also writes odd bits of high fantasy with swords and orcs. In addition, he is the Editor and Publisher of *Boundary Shock Quarterly Magazine*. You can find out more at his website www.blazeward.com, as well as Facebook, Goodreads, and other places.

Blaze's works are available as ebooks, paper, and audio, and can be found at a variety of online vendors. His newsletter comes out quarterly, and you can also follow his blog on his website. He really enjoys interacting with fans, and looks forward to any and all questions—even ones about his books!

Never miss a release!
If you'd like to be notified of new releases, sign up
for my newsletter.

I will never spam you or use your email for nefarious purposes. You can also unsubscribe at any time.

http://www.blazeward.com/newsletter/

Connect with Blaze!

Web: www.blazeward.com
Boundary Shock Quarterly (BSQ):
https://www.boundaryshockquarterly.com/

facebook.com/KRPBlaze

goodreads.com/Blaze_Ward

ABOUT KNOTTED ROAD PRESS

Knotted Road Press fiction specializes in dynamic writing set in mysterious, exotic locations.

Knotted Road Press non-fiction publishes autobiographies, business books, cookbooks, and how-to books with unique voices.

Knotted Road Press creates DRM-free ebooks as well as high-quality print books for readers around the world.

With authors in a variety of genres including literary, poetry, mystery, fantasy, and science fiction, Knotted Road Press has something for everyone.

Knotted Road Press
www.KnottedRoadPress.com